EUREKA PUBLIC LIBRARY
A66200 743264

D1115148

CHANGES of HEART

PAIGE LEE ELLISTON

Grand Rapids, Michigan

Published by Fleming H. Revell
a division of Baker Publishing Group
P.O. Box 6287, Grand Rapids, MI 49516-6287

Printed in the United States of America

Library of Congress Cataloging-in-Publication Data

Elliston, Paige Lee.
Changes of heart / Paige Lee Elliston.
p. cm. — (Montana skies ; bk. 1)
ISBN 0-8007-5939-7
1. Women—Montana—Fiction. 2. Loss (Psychology)—Fiction. 3. Ranch life—Fiction. 4. Montana—Fiction. I. Title.
PS3065.L4755C47 2005
813′.6—dc22 2004029416

1

Maggie tugged the heavy sheepskin coat around her body as she hustled from her house to the barn. There wasn't much wind, but what breeze did exist had cruel, arctic arrogance that numbed her face and made her gloveless fingers tingle. Her western boots made the snow squeak as she walked on it, and the cold penetrated her jeans.

In spite of the temperature and the shiver that had already started her teeth clattering against one another, Maggie stopped ten or so yards from the barn and took in a deep breath. The air was achingly cold in her throat, in her lungs, but it was so pristine and so unsullied by civilization and its contaminants that it made her think of the air eight, ten, and more miles above the earth, where Rich flew—the foothills of outer space, as he called it.

She took another breath and looked to the sky. Stars were said to be much bigger in Montana than anywhere else—they gleamed and shimmered with a pure white radiance that was almost painful to the eye—and they seemed close enough for her to reach up and touch them.

"Maggie! Come on—we need you!"

The front sliding doors of the big barn were open a foot or so, and through the gap Maggie saw Rich, her husband of six years. He stood at the support beam that had the intercom attached to it, his thumb pressing against the button that created a raucous buzz in the house. Next to him stood a standard fifty-five-gallon polyethylene barrel painted a sparkling and flawless white. On it were emblazoned the letters NBRA in eye-searing Day-Glo red. Under the letters, in a smaller font, was the line "National Barrel Racing Association."

Maggie watched Rich for a moment, a grin breaking across her face. He still hadn't figured out how to use the intercom properly, apparently not realizing that every time he pressed the button, the buzz sawed away any words he may have been speaking, and all that could be heard in the house was incoherent, excited gibberish.

He flies forty-seven million dollar test aircraft, and he can't figure out a basic Radio Shack communications hookup, she thought. Her grin became a full smile. The cockpit of the X-417 flashed in her mind; it had more dials and gauges and flip switches and buttons than a nuclear power plant. Rich knew precisely what each one was for, and his fingers found them as unerringly as a skilled surgeon finds a bleeding artery. But a simple intercom . . .

She watched Rich for a bit longer. His hair, blond as a fresh bale of prime straw, was disheveled, as if he'd been running his hands through it. He wasn't tall for a man—standing five foot nine—but he gave the impression of height because of his lean, whipcord-tough body and his almost military posture. Her husband looked, Maggie believed, like a recruiting poster for the Boy Scouts of America.

Maggie pushed through the door. "What's up?"

Rich spoke into the microphone of the unit. "Hurry! She's—"Then he realized that his wife was standing behind him and spun to face her. "She's pacing around the stall a lot, and she seems nervous or scared or something. I offered her a carrot, and she hardly sniffed it. I don't like this. Her eyes aren't right. Suppose . . ."

"Of course she's nervous and excited, Richie. It's her first foal. All this is brand new to her." She put her hand lightly on his arm. "This is all natural stuff, honey. I appreciate all your concern, and I know you love Dusty, but your hovering over her is probably making her more nervous than she needs to be. Besides, God did a great job when he arranged how horses are born; he really doesn't need you supervising."

Their eyes met. "She . . . she wants me there, Maggie. She really does."

It was a little boy's remark, and it made the back of Maggie's throat suddenly sore with the love it expressed. She could feel tears beginning in her eyes. She stepped forward and hugged her husband. "Of course she does," she said, her voice husky. "Let's go take a look."

The barn wasn't quite three years old, but it had already taken on the scents of a well-maintained equine structure. The smell of the creosoted beams—for the first year, strong and acrid with the taint of kerosene—was now barely noticeable, and what remained was a rich, full odor that spoke of the strength and permanence of the wood. Maggie took a deep breath and took in the scent of oiled leather, a unique aroma, and to horse people such as herself, as delicate and sensual as the most costly French perfume. Adding to the distinctive scent of the barn was the fresh, springlike smell of healthy horse hides, and the crimped oats and molasses, timothy hay, and new straw.

The smile returned to Maggie's face as she followed Rich down the center aisle. A dozen and more curious horses watched the two people pass from individual box stalls, and many of the animals nickered for a treat or a scratch behind the ears. The sheer joy of the moment—her loving and beloved husband's concern for first-time mother Dusty, the wonders of the Montana prairie, the barn and the house—brought a frequently used prayer to Maggie's mind: *My cup runneth over, Lord. Thank you for all this.*

The birthing stall was at the end of the barn, separated from the main section and the other horses. Unlike most of the stalls, this one had no window and was slightly smaller than the others. Maggie had explained to Rich that many pregnant mares pace as their time comes closer, and too much room could allow them to move too quickly, tangle their hooves because of the unbalanced foals they carry, and fall, hurting themselves and their babies.

Two heat lamps perched in the corners of the birthing stall cast amber light on the bay quarter horse mare that stood facing the stall gate. Maggie stepped around her husband. "You know, Richie," she said with a laugh, "if you call me out here again on a false alarm, our Christmas Eve dinner is going to turn to ash, and we'll be late for . . ."

Maggie stepped closer to the stall and looked into eyes that were wide and unfocused, the usual glinting chestnut now flat and dull. "Oh, Dusty," she exclaimed, fumbling with the latch on the stall. She swung the gate open and rushed to the horse, her right hand feeling for the pulse point at the mare's throat. Dusty's skin was much warmer than it should have been, and a slick patina of sweat coated her chest and neck. Her pulse was rapid but erratic, throbbing insanely fast, stopping for a moment, and then racing again. A hissing, spattering sound came from the rear and under the mare, and her body began to tremble. A metallic, foul smell reached Maggie, and she crouched, peering under the horse. It wasn't urine Dusty was voiding—it was blood, great spurts of scarlet liquid that issued from her birth canal, saturating the white gauze that wrapped her tail and spraying against the boards of the back of the enclosure.

"Richie, call Dr. Pulver now! Tell him it's an emergency—life and death—and that Dusty is fevered, her pulse is bouncing and very accelerated, and that she's spraying uterine blood. Run, honey—or we're going to lose Dusty!"

Danny Pulver, DVM, weary after a long day of barn calls, tossed a Milk-Bone to his collie, Sunday. Christmas music—some carols but primarily longer symphonic pieces from the small Coldwater FM station—wafted through his small home as he leaned against his kitchen counter and gnawed on a ham sandwich.

His cell phone vibrated in his pocket. "Merry Christmas," he said, "Dan Pulver speaking."

Rich's voice was rushed, his words running together. "Dusty's in trouble. She's bleeding terribly. Maggie said we need you, Dan."

The smile left the vet's face as if it had been suddenly slapped away. "Easy, Rich. Slow down and take me through what happened. Is Dusty standing? How much blood is she losing? From where?"

Rich took a breath, but his voice remained shaky. "It's coming from her birth canal. She's standing and tries to bite at her gut and she's groaning. Her chest is all sweaty. She's—"

"OK, Rich. Look—tell Maggie that if the mare wants to go down to let her do so, but try to keep her from writhing until I get there. Maggie's a good hand with horses. She needs you to calm down and be ready to help. Do what she tells you. I'm on my way."

Dr. Pulver grabbed his medical satchel from its place by the door and ran to his GMC 4x4. Sunday ran next to him, but Danny waved the dog back. He put his key in the ignition, hauled on his shoulder belt, and tromped on the gas pedal. The big V-8 engine hurtled the vehicle forward, knobby tires smoking as they clawed for traction.

Danny calculated the time it would take to get to the Lockes' little ranch. During the day it was an easy twenty-minute drive. On Christmas Eve, with traffic essentially nonexistent this far out in the wilds, he could make it in ten. There'd been some light snow earlier in the day, but the road was clear and there wasn't much danger from ice—the temperature hadn't gone over eight degrees in several days and there'd been almost no snow—and the moon was full, with good visibility. Danny glanced down at his speedometer—a bit over sixty miles per hour—and applied some more pressure to the accelerator.

He'd met Rich and Maggie Locke a little more than a year ago at a church festival when he'd first opened his practice. New clients were hard to come by in the area. Most of the cattlemen and the horse people seemed satisfied with the veterinarians from the established vet hospital in Coldwater, the nearest town. The folks who ran barrels or roped from their mounts in competition or showed their animals at halter or in pleasure classes were very particular about who took care of their horses' health. Danny's specialty was equine medicine, but he'd been seeing mostly dogs, cats, birds, and the occasional snake before Maggie gave him her business.

She was a stunner. When she'd approached him at the festival and introduced herself, his eyes had swept to her left hand, and he'd swallowed a lump of disappointment when he'd seen her wedding band. She was perhaps five foot five, and her brown eyes had a warmth to them that made it impossible not to smile when speaking with her. Her chestnut hair reached to her shoulders and was all the more attractive because she didn't fuss with it. In fact, Danny figured she probably hadn't seen the inside of a beauty salon in years; hers was a natural beauty that didn't need curling irons or hairspray or makeup to manifest itself.

Danny clicked on the high beams of the already-powerful halogen headlamps, and the sweep of light deepened ahead of him. A pair of strangely green eyes, reflecting light like polished jewels, appeared to the right, perhaps fifty yards ahead. Almost immediately another pair appeared—and then another. Danny's foot tapped the brake pedal as the group of deer—nine or ten of them, at least—moved onto the narrow shoulder of the road and stood gawking at him, obviously mesmerized by the brilliant lights bearing down on them.

Danny jammed the steering wheel to the left, at the same time stomping the antilock brake pedal. The knobby, fatly treaded tires screamed in protest as the rear end of the GMC broke traction and slid to the right, the howl of the rubber and the shrill scream of the decelerating engine a cacophony in the cab of the truck. Danny eased the steering wheel into the skid, felt the magic point where he was again in control, and down-shifted into third gear. Again, the vehicle threatened to slide, but this time to the left, where Danny wanted it. He touched the accelerator with his toe, feeding a bit more power to the engine and using the huge V-8 to neutralize the skid, and rocketed past the cluster of deer that gaped at the truck as it blasted past them, less than a yard away from the lead buck's nose. Safe again in his own lane, the veterinarian wiped sweat from his forehead with the back of a hand and stepped again on the accelerator.

Dusty was down on her side, her bay coat slick with sweat, when Danny dashed into the barn, his bag of equipment at his side. He shoved past Rich and nodded to him without speaking, seeing the depth of the fear in the man's eyes. Maggie, crouched at the mare's rear, her hands bloody and her face streaked with tears that glittered in the light, was yet more frightened than her husband. "Danny," she rasped. "She . . ."

Danny dropped his bag, worked the latch, and slid his hands into a pair of latex gloves. "Let me in there, Maggie," he said, already lowering himself in front of the woman. He concentrated as his trained fingers palpated the depths of the groaning mare's reproductive organs. A barely felt sensation—that of a tiny fingertip tapping on the back of his right hand—froze his movements. He waited a full ten seconds, focusing on the rhythmic pulsing, and then, sure that what he was feeling was blood escaping a torn umbilical cord, eased his hands into a better position. Dusty squealed as he did so, and Danny cringed, but he had no other course. Causing this fine mare some pain now could save her life and that of her foal. He followed the cord with his fingers, its sleek, warm length amazing him as it always did. The words of his Cornell University professor of anatomy's words played in his mind: "The umbilical cord isn't merely a messenger of life—it is life itself. It's the tie between all of those who have come before and all of those who are to be."

The vet's finger found the leak, lost it for a second, found it again, and followed the sinuous path of the cord to the foal's stomach. The problem quickly became clear: the rupture was the result of a twist around the foal's forefoot—the umbilical cord had stretched and then had partially split, probably because of movements of the mare, the foal, or both.

Danny's fingers told him the foal was alive, and his face broke into a relieved grin as he looked over his shoulder at Maggie and Rich. "We're not going to lose Mama tonight," he said. "And we're going to have a live birth here before too long."

For the briefest part of a moment, the eyes of the young couple brought to Danny's mind the image of the deer eyes he'd seen not twenty minutes ago, but then the fear disappeared and the faces of the man and woman glowed with joy and relief.

Contractions started again almost immediately. Dusty's hindquarters tensed, her muscles as rigid as bands of steel—and then Danny held a foal in his arms. Again, his hands moved quickly and surely, pulling a messy knot of greenish mucus from the baby's nostrils, wiping afterbirth from the eyes, feeling for spinal structure, listening to the first breath the animal drew. He eased his little finger into the foal's mouth, and when the intrusion was greeted, after a heartbeat, with a strong suckling instinct, Danny knew he was crying—just as he did each time he attended a successful birth.

And he wasn't alone. Tears of happiness and gratitude—

and awe at the miracle of birth—streamed down the faces of Rich and Maggie Locke as well.

Even with the by-products of birth adhering to the foal's coat, the color was apparent. He was a red chestnut, and there was a jagged snippet of white on his muzzle.

The heady, delightfully rich aroma of strong, freshly brewed coffee filled Maggie's kitchen the way sunshine fills a perfect July day. Maggie's Christmas roast, now like a small cinder block that'd spent a day in a blast furnace, was wrapped in newspaper on the counter, a gift for Danny's collie, Sunday. Maggie, Rich, and Danny's faces were flushed from the hours they'd spent in the cold, as well as from the giddy excitement each of them felt.

"What are you going to name him?" Danny asked, sipping coffee.

"Well," Maggie said, "his name with the Quarter Horse Registry will be 'Lancer's Quick Prince,' because the stud was from the Lancer line and Dusty's registered name is 'Far Away Princess.' We'd already decided on that—if he was a male."

Rich snorted. "Is there anything more pretentious than the registered names you horse people come up with?" He laughed, grinning at Maggie. "Can you imagine standing in the paddock in the morning, calling, 'Here, Lancer's Quick Prince?'"

"Hush, you. If you're so clever, why don't you name him?"

Rich didn't hesitate. "Dancer."

"Dancer?" Maggie and Danny asked in unison.

"You betcha. Look: first of all, if it wasn't for Danny, we wouldn't have the foal, correct? So, we incorporate the first part of Danny's name. And then—did you see how the cute little guy stood on those stick legs?"

"I'll admit I'm cute, but there's nothing wrong with my legs," Danny said.

"I meant the foal, you narcissist."

"It still applies, narcissist or not."

Maggie laughed. *How has a guy like this—good looking, bright, funny, and a genuinely compassionate veterinarian—remained unmarried?*

"Come on!" Rich said. "I'm serious—when that baby was poking around for Dusty's nipple, did you see how his feet moved? So gracefully, as if he'd practiced it? Dancer is a perfect name for him."

A moment passed. "You know," Danny said, "Rich has a real good point about the way the foal moved."

"Dancer it is," Maggie said, rising from her chair and moving to her husband to embrace him. "Great name," she said. "He'll be the best barrel-racing horse ever." She met Danny's eyes. "Thank you," she said quietly.

"Yeah," Rich added. "Thanks, Danny."

Maggie awakened shortly before 5:00 the next morning. Her husband was already gone; his side of their bed was cold under her hand. She'd known he wouldn't be there when she woke up—it was part of a ritual they'd established whenever Rich was flying a new, untested aircraft.

After they'd checked Dusty and Dancer one final time the night before and come back to the house, Rich had put the jeans and shirt he'd put on the next morning on one of the kitchen chairs. Neither of them spoke of what he was doing—there'd been tears and stilted conversations and a palpable tension the first few times Rich had piloted untried planes. It was terribly hard on both of them—particularly Maggie. They'd had to find a solution. Fortunately, Maggie was a sound sleeper—once she was out for the night, an earthquake couldn't wake her. Rich slept like a feral cat, leaving sleep quickly, ready to do what needed to be done, immediately in full command of all his senses. So they decided that on the days he would be flying untried planes, he would leave very early in the morning, before Maggie woke up.

A small smile began to form on Maggie's face as she swung her feet out from under the covers. The first time Rich had snuck out of their bed to pilot a jet fighter that was more like a rocket than an airplane, he'd left a note on the kitchen table for her in his neat, almost surgically precise handwriting.

> Dear Maggie:
> It's like driving a bus, honey. No sweat. What's for lunch?
> I love you,
> Rich

Maggie knew there'd be another note, worded exactly the same way, on the table this morning. She had an even dozen of them neatly folded in her jewelry box. On each, a random letter or even a full word was slightly smeared from where her tears had fallen on it. Rich didn't know that, and she never planned to tell him about how such mornings almost tore the heart out of her—how she begged the Lord to bring him back to her safely this time, just as he had in the past.

She saw the note on the table but didn't immediately go to pick it up. The kitchen, with its brightly polished maple table and gleaming pots and pans hung over the stove, shimmered in her vision. She shut her eyes, forcing away the tears. The lights on the Christmas tree—which Rich had turned on before he left—seemed to mock her with the peace and joy they represented. The wrapped gifts they'd exchange later were piled neatly at the base of the tree, but the glossy sheen of the silver and red gift wrap did nothing to counter the strange feeling of dread she was experiencing.

Christmas morning and they've got to do this—they've got to fly that thing. Rich had explained how the new fuel mixture—some top-secret stuff—had a very short life and needed to be used almost immediately or its chemical composition would change, and how the plane itself had to be secured in a hangar with a half dozen armed special forces personnel guarding it at all times, and how the atmospheric conditions were perfect . . . and so forth.

What is it with these men? she thought. *They're like little boys competing to see whose bike is fastest or who can climb the highest tree. Always faster—always higher.* They laughed about what they did—they goaded one another, and then they would stand there in their full-dress uniforms while another one of them was buried. At the wake they'd give their sympathy to the widow and then cluster outside and talk about the top-secret plane Lockheed or Boeing or some such firm was building.

Maggie shook her head angrily, and it was then she noticed that her fists were clenched so tightly that her fingernails had drawn blood from her palms. For a long moment, she gazed at her right hand as if she'd never seen it before, her eyes following the tiny trickles of blood. Then, woodenly, she walked to the sink to wash her hands, her lips moving as she prayed. *Please, Lord, bring him back this time.*

She turned to the table and picked up the note and was immediately shamed by the flash of anger she'd just experienced. The words on the scrap of paper were exactly the same as they'd been on the others, but at the bottom of this one was a stick-legged sketch of a foal with musical notes floating in the air around it and little lines indicating that the legs were moving . . . dancing.

Just like him, she thought, a grin tugging at the corners of her mouth. The perspective—the point of view—of a boy in a fully grown man's body.

She recalled one of their conversations about the new plane and propulsion system he was testing this day.

"It's a real leap in technology, and that's the important thing, Maggie. Our country has millions and millions of dollars and thousands of hours of research and development into the X-417. America needs this plane to keep it safe, to keep it strong. My part in all that is tiny—I just steer the thing. The scientists and the engineers are the real heroes."

Then he'd added sheepishly, "'Course, the fact that going at twice the speed of sound is absolutely a ton of fun might enter into it too."

Maggie did her best to hold on to that image as she pulled on jeans, a sweater, boots, and her sheepskin coat. As she hurried from the house to the barn through the almost arctic chill in the pristine air, her senses were assaulted by a roaring, high-pitched shriek that seemed too loud and too piercing for even the vastness of the Montana sky to contain. The X-417 looked more like a dart than an airplane, and as she stared upward, the silly-looking stubby wings rocked back and forth in a salute to her. Then the aircraft seemed to stand on its tail for a heartbeat and rocketed straight upward like a bolt fired from a gigantic crossbow. Brilliant bright-blue flames appeared at the tail for the tiniest part of a second, and the scream of the engine threatened to deafen her. Before she could get her hands to her ears, Maggie lost the plane in the face of the morning sun.

Dusty nickered as Maggie approached the birthing stall. Maggie had expected the mare to instinctively put her body between Maggie and the foal, but Dusty greeted her owner like a proud mother, licking the noisily nursing foal and then finding Maggie's eyes with her own.

"You should be proud, Dusty," Maggie said with a laugh. "He's a beautiful baby—a perfect baby."

Dancer's head popped out from under his mother at the sound of Maggie's voice. He had the typical big-eyed, surprised look of all foals. His coat, after hours of Dusty's licking, gleamed like burnished brass, and the snippet of white midpoint on his muzzle was as pure a white as new snow. He stared at Maggie for a long moment, huffed wetly through his nostrils, and ducked back under his mother to find the nipple he'd left. As he shifted his body, Maggie noticed that the walking-on-stilts, tangled-leg shakiness that a youngster not a full day old would normally exhibit was conspicuously absent. Dancer shifted his hips easily and smoothly, and his forefeet followed with the same grace.

Dusty poked her muzzle toward Maggie, asking for a treat, and Maggie scratched behind the mare's ears. "Of course a new mama needs a carrot," Maggie whispered. "I'm so proud of you, Dusty."

She turned away to the basket of carrots on the floor, selected a large one, and wiped the grit and dirt from it on her jeans. She was turning back to Dusty when a whistling shriek tore the peace to sharp-edged shards. Less than a full second later the entire barn trembled, windows rattling, beams and boards groaning as a massive shock wave assaulted the structure. The explosion was far too loud to be called a mere sound—it was a palpable and physical cataclysm that slammed into Maggie like an unexpected kick to the stomach. She dropped the carrot and ran frantically to the front of the barn and outside, unaware that she was screaming.

A white contrail pointed from the depths of the sky straight to the ground, where a red-orange fireball spread upward in a ferociously burning, roiling, deadly fist.

2

The church in Coldwater had survived an attack in 1877 by a band of marauding post–Civil War night riders, in which the men of the town turned away the wild-eyed horsemen by firing at them from inside the church through rifle slits cut into the heavy wooden shutters for just such a purpose. The church had stood, strong and resolute, through the First and Second World Wars, the Korean conflict, and the Vietnam War. It had withstood and triumphed over televangelist hucksters, free love, and New Age crystals.

And in the past dozen years the church had held memorial services for three test pilots. The service this day was for Rich Locke. A sea of USAF full-dress uniforms occupied the pews, as did almost as many ill-fitting and rarely worn suits and strangely configured tie-knots of the ranchers, horse people, barrel racers, trail riders, and calf ropers who knew the Lockes. The pilots wore spit-polished black shoes; the others wore Western boots. More than a few of the Justins, Tony Lamas, and custom-made boots were still damp from the process of hosing off horse manure to get them ready for the service. The two rear pews held women from the ages of fifteen to perhaps fifty-five who were dressed sedately in Western-cut dresses. Most of the ladies wore small silver pins with the letters NBRA on them.

Ms. Elspeth Traynor stood in front of the altar in a black robe, one hand holding her Bible, the other resting on the aluminum walker in front of her. Reverend Helmut Traynor, who had died more than a year ago, was as much a part of the church as the wood and mortar and stained glass, even in death. His wife, Ellie, as she was known to the congregation, was now approaching her seventy-sixth birthday. She'd come to Coldwater with her husband immediately after he completed divinity school, and neither one of them had left since that day. The search for a minister had begun shortly after Helmut's death, but the people of Coldwater had begged Ellie to stay on in the ministerial home and continue with her church work at least until a new shepherd was found.

The lapel microphone on Ellie's robe was a recent concession to her age, but with its amplification, her voice reached every part of the old church, rich and true, although at times tremulous as emotion overcame her.

"How I wish Helmut were here to comfort all of us," Ellie said. "But we all know where Helmut walks now—and we know that Richie Locke walks with him." She paused. "There'll be no sermon today, nor will there be a eulogy as such, at least not from me. I'm not qualified to present either. But I can say this to you, my friends: Richie was loved—is loved—because of the man he was, a humble child of the

Lord, a wonderful husband, and a protector of our great country who died doing what he devoutly believed was his duty and his mission in life."

Only the quiet sobs of Maggie Locke disturbed the solemn quiet in Coldwater Church. Ellie's voice broke again as she opened her Bible. "Let us pray together . . ."

". . . So here I am at sixty-five thousand feet, pulling almost three g's at the top of a loop, with the fire light goin' crazy and the system's warning honker blasting in my ears, and here's my wingman drifting toward me like he's asleep or something . . ." The young pilot held his hands a little above shoulder height, moving them slowly together a foot apart, his left moving closer to his right as he scribed an arc in the air. The cluster of other men, the silver wings on their shoulders glinting in the bright sunlight, leaned forward toward the speaker, their eyes locked on his hands.

"You guys know how shaky the stabilizer on the Thunder-Bolt 336 is, right?" Heads nodded, and a couple of the pilots grunted.

"Well, all I could do was keep the power at max and try to engage my—"

Maggie and her parents walked around the end of the Toole van. The speaker's hand froze in the air in front of him. The heads of the flyers turned to Maggie, their faces like those of a band of little boys caught smoking cigarettes behind the barn.

"Maggie . . ." one said. "We . . . uhhh . . ."

Maggie's voice was harsh, raspy, and she felt as if she were tearing the words from her heart and throwing them at the uniformed men. "I didn't even have a body to bury! There was nothing left of Rich but black smoke and the stink of that fuel. And you . . . you stupid, selfish children stand out here playing airplane! How can you—"

"Maggie," her father said gently, taking her arm and leading her away from the stunned and silent group of pilots. Janice Stuart, Maggie's mother, put her arm around her daughter's waist, helping to move her away toward the Stuarts' vehicle. "Come on, honey," Janice said. "Let's go home."

Maggie had been physically present throughout the service for Rich, but it was as if her body were a poorly functioning but automatic machine and her mind was stuck in a loop of images of her husband—his smile, the manner in which he used his hands as he spoke, the spontaneity of his love for her that so frequently ignited in his eyes for no particular reason, the way his hand so sweetly and unselfconsciously found hers when they walked together.

Brad Stuart clicked his key fob, and the automatic locks of the Mercedes SUV popped open with a metallic snap. He opened the rear passenger door, and Maggie slumped inside, choking against tears and her sudden anger at the men who had been Rich's colleagues and friends. Janice followed her daughter into the car, tugging Maggie to her, enveloping her, wiping away her tears with her fingers. "We'll get through this, baby. You'll see," Janice whispered. She held Maggie tighter as Maggie's body convulsed and her voice choked out bits of indistinguishable words.

Brad walked around the SUV to the driver's seat. He hesitated a moment before opening the door. He was a wealthy man—the owner of more than a dozen "Get Rollin'" auto tune-up and repair facilities—and he'd never felt quite so helpless in his life.

Maggie was his and Janice's only child, and they'd raised her with perhaps too many things and too much money, but despite that, the girl had a flinty foundation of independence. Maggie had babysat as a kid and had worked a few hours a day at a local bakery all through high school. She agreed to borrow two thousand dollars from Brad when she was fifteen to buy her first horse, although she'd been riding since she was seven. She paid the loan back in weekly increments over three years, without missing a single payment. He'd accepted Maggie's payments each week with more than a little pride in his child's spirit.

That was one of the reasons Rich's almost frantic call ten days ago continued to trouble Brad. "I can't tell Maggie, Brad—I can't," Rich had said, his voice low, almost a whisper. "But this plane I'm going to fly in a week is powered by a brand-new fuel that's going to revolutionize jet air travel. I mean it—and there was an opportunity to buy into the fuel provider. It's not insider stuff—it's all legal and aboveboard, and lots of my friends are buying the stock. It's a way for Maggie and me to get out from under our mortgage and pay off the barn and have more operating capital for Maggie's horse operation. It can't miss, Brad—I give you my word on that."

"The ones that can't miss are the ones that bury people, son. You know that. There's no such thing as a sure thing in the market."

There was a pause, and then Rich's voice became a tad louder and more assertive. "Brad," he said, "I wouldn't tell you how to run your stores. I know jet engines and flying as well as you know auto repair. This will be a short-term loan—after I fly that plane with the new fuel, the aviation market is going to go berserk. I know this, sir. I know it."

"How deep are you in, Rich? You must've taken a big bite if you need money for basic operating expenses."

"Well . . . yeah. I'm in up to my ears."

"How much, son?"

"I . . . I'd rather not give you a number. The thing is, I refinanced the house and barn, used our savings, sold what little stock we had—the whole smash. I even borrowed against the value of the insurance policy the Air Force carries on me. It amounts to nothing until I pay back the loan."

Brad struggled to bite off his quick reply. After a moment, he said, "And you did all this without Maggie knowing? Do you feel right about that?"

"Yeah, Brad, I do. This is going to surprise her. It'll be the biggest surprise of her life. I came into our marriage with next to nothing. It took me years to pay off my mom's hospital bills. But now, with this opportunity, Maggie can buy more horses, buy the six-stall trailer for when she's campaigning her stock, and buy whatever else she needs. I owe this to Maggie. I really do—and I'm going to see that it happens for her, no matter what."

"Rich . . . you've got to understand that I'm not questioning what you want to do for Maggie—and it's not the money, either. I have it and you and Maggie will end up with it anyway, after Jan and I are gone. But I can't do this behind my daughter's back. She's got to know about the loan, and approve of it. I'm sorry, but I can't do a thing unless we agree to that condition."

Again, Rich's words were rapid. "The only way this thing can get messed up is if I drive the X-417 straight into the ground—and that's not going to happen. I know that aircraft like Maggie knows her horses—better, probably. Animals can get nutsy, but machines can't."

"I'm not doubting your skills, son. I know you'll make that plane do precisely what you want it to—just as you have with the other ones. That's not the point. It's just that I can't do this behind . . . Look—can you hold out until Christmas Day? Jan and I'll be there midday at the latest. Can we talk then?"

Rich's response was a bit slow in coming. "Sure—that'll be fine. By the time you get to our place I'll be back from Toole, with the test flight behind me. We'll talk then, OK?"

What sounded like a tornado approaching from the west snapped Brad Stuart's eyes to the sky. The sound became a high-pitched, screeching, all-encompassing roar, and five jet fighters in a tight V formation blasted toward the church. Directly over the building they turned sharply upward, the needle-noses of the planes seeking the upper reaches of the universe, the creamy white contrails strikingly defined against the cobalt blue of the sky. The space to the right of and below the lead jet was conspicuously and quite solemnly vacant—the pilot's salute to a fallen comrade.

In the SUV Maggie moaned and hugged her head with frantic hands. Janice held Maggie, rocking her gently, as if she were an infant. "We'll get through this, honey."

Brad sat behind the steering wheel and thunked the heavy door closed. His eyes met those of his wife in the rearview mirror, and he wondered for a long moment if what Janice had said contained any bit of truth at all.

Maggie leaned up against the birthing stall and stared at the new foal. In his eight days of life, Dancer had shown more personality than most foals did in their first couple of months. He was a curious animal. His chestnut, almost black, eyes flicked toward every new sound or voice, and his ears were in almost constant motion, pointing at whatever caught his attention. Dancer didn't display the natural and normal hesitancy of a very young horse. He didn't slide behind or next to his mother when people came to their stall, keeping her body between him and those strange creatures that walked upright. Instead, he moved toward rather than away from a hand held out to him and seemed to take great delight when his muzzle was gently stroked or his poll—the spot between his ears—lightly rubbed.

Maggie spent a few hours every day at or in the birthing

stall. It was there she felt a sense of peace that she couldn't find elsewhere. But even with her horses, she found no joy. She felt Rich's death physically, as if she carried the invisible but ponderously weighty pelt of some huge animal on her back and shoulders. She'd lost a dozen pounds from her already lean frame, and her jeans hung from her waist like they were two sizes too large for her, even though her belt was buckled at its final increment. She lived on coffee and whatever her mother was able to get her to eat.

Maggie didn't realize that her father had come up behind her at the stall until she felt his hand on her shoulder and heard his voice.

She turned to face him, a forced smile beginning to mold her face.

"Don't," Brad said. "Don't try to smile, honey. You've never been phony in your life, and now isn't the time to start."

Maggie nodded and turned back to her horses. Dancer moved closer, muzzle raised a bit, trying the scent of Maggie's father. When Dancer recognized it, he snuffed and moved a step closer to the man and woman, seeking Brad's usual light touch. This time, for once, Brad ignored the foal.

"There are some things we need to talk about, Maggie," Brad said. "I need to get back to my stores in a few days. Your mom is going to stay on for as long as she needs to. I'll do my best to fly out on weekends."

"It's not necessary for Mom to—"

Brad cleared his throat. "Whether it's necessary or not, she's staying, and I don't want you to try to dissuade her.

Her heart is breaking right along with yours, and she needs to be with you, needs to be your mother." His voice became stronger. "Don't shut her out, Maggie."

"I'm sorry," Maggie whispered.

"Don't be sorry, either, baby. Believe me, I know how you feel and how you—"

"No, you don't, Dad. Mom never died and left you alone."

Brad sighed. "No. She didn't. I'm sorry; I shouldn't have said that. But we're worried about you. You're losing weight you can't spare. You're eating next to nothing. You pace the house all night long, you won't pray with us, and you won't see the friends who stop by to visit you. Grief is grief, honey—and it's the most painful thing in the world—but you've got to smooth some of the sharp edges away."

"My life is over, Dad."

Her father turned her away from the stall to face him, his grip firm but lovingly gentle. He used his right hand to lift her chin, forcing her to meet his eyes. "It isn't, Maggie. I've never known you to be a quitter. What happened to Richie is a horrible tragedy, but you can't allow it to destroy you. That isn't what Richie would want, and it's not what your mother and I want, either. I know only a week has gone by, but I—we—are really frightened by what we're seeing. C'mon, let's go inside and talk with your mom. OK?"

They walked together to the house, her father's arm protectively around her waist. Halfway there, Maggie moved her own arm to her father's midsection, and it stayed there until they reached the steps.

"I'm not a quitter," Maggie said, her hand on the doorknob.

"I know that, baby."

Janice was sitting at the kitchen table when Maggie and her father came in from outside. Janice had a neat stack of condolence cards and personal letters in front of her and a half dozen or so other pieces of mail that she rather clumsily attempted to cover with her arm. "I thought I'd separate the mail, honey—set aside the ones you'll want to answer." She stood and swept up the mail she'd been attempting to conceal into a quick, sloppy pile and picked it up. One envelope with a lurid red "Third Notice" stamped on its face dropped to the table. Before her mother could snatch up the letter, the words registered in Maggie's mind.

"What in the world is this?" she asked, reaching toward the envelope.

"Junk mail and stuff and nonsense," Janice said hurriedly. "You don't need to concern yourself with it right now." She forced a smile. "How about I put a fresh pot of coffee on?"

Maggie tore open the envelope and scanned the letter. Her face flushed with quick anger. "This is impossible! We've never missed a mortgage payment! Richie pays everything on the first of each month—this is a big mistake." She looked at her father in panic. She didn't like what she saw.

Her dad sighed. "No, it isn't, Maggie. I'm sorry. I was waiting for the right time to discuss this with you." He paused for a moment. "Sit down, OK?"

"Brad . . ." Janice began.

"There is no good time, Jan," Brad said. "I guess now is as good as any. C'mon, honey, sit down. You too, Jan."

"I won't sit down!" Maggie held the letter in front of her like a challenging sword, her hot glare focused on her father. "What's going on here? What's this all about?"

"Calm down," Brad said gently, easing himself into a chair at the table. "Yelling at me isn't going to accomplish anything. Let's talk about this."

Maggie held her father's eyes with her own for a long moment and then stiffly moved a chair out from the table and sat down, her posture rigid, the letter still clutched in her hand. After a moment, Jan sat too.

"I got a call from Rich about a week before Christmas. He needed money. I don't know how else to say this. He did a very . . . well . . . misguided thing. He did it for you, honey—I completely believe that. But it was a foolish thing to do."

Maggie began to speak, but her father held up his hand to quiet her.

"Let me tell you the whole thing. Then we'll discuss it. OK?"

Very slowly, Maggie nodded her head.

It didn't take long to tell.

The color of anger drained from Maggie's face very quickly, leaving her with a sickly white pallor. Her hand released the letter, and parts of the text were smeared from the nervous sweat of her palm. The silence in the kitchen became an oppressive force.

Jan cleared her throat. "Rich did it for you, Maggie. We all know he didn't lust after money for itself—this crazy investment thing was to be a gift to you, to help you expand your career with your horses, to make sure you wanted for nothing."

"Well," Maggie said. Then, after a long moment of silence, she added, "He didn't tell me, though. We always told each other everything, but he didn't tell me about this."

"That was wrong, Maggie—but you had to hear his voice at the beginning of his call to me to understand it," Brad said. "He was as excited as I was when I bought your first bicycle and kept it hidden in our bedroom closet until Christmas morning. Your mother was sure I was going to give it away—and every time I saw you, I almost did. That's how Richie felt—like he was doing something loving and wonderful for you."

As Maggie began to speak, Jan leaned across the table and took her daughter's hand. "Let me say something here. There are two ways you can go with this, Maggie." Maggie turned to look at her mother. Brad did as well. His wife wasn't an aggressive woman, but she was a strong and clear-thinking Christian with a rock-hard faith that made her counsel well worth hearing.

"You can torture yourself with what Richie did, and worry and cry and wonder what the man was thinking by not discussing his plan with you. You can make the whole thing bigger than it is in your mind and in your heart, and let it chew away at you for the rest of your life. Or . . ." Janice paused. "Or you can accept it for what it was: a surprise gift from your husband that went terribly, tragically wrong. And you can hold that in your heart—how much he loved you—and let it bring joy to you until you join him at the end of your own life. It's up to you, honey. Dad and I can take care of the money for you with no problem. I'm much more concerned about how you—"

"No," Maggie said with a voice that was more alive than it had been since Christmas day. "What you said is true, Mom, and thanks for saying it. But the money is my problem now, and I'll take care of it without a handout from you and Dad."

Brad reached into his jacket pocket and removed a neatly folded check. "We've been very fortunate, honey. Business is good. This"—he gestured with the check—"won't be missed or needed. Can't you let us help you? Isn't that what parents do for their children?"

Maggie pushed her chair back, stood, and stepped to her father. She leaned and kissed his cheek. "Thank you so much, Daddy—but no. I can't and won't accept it." She stood straight again, and some of the color came back in her face. "I've got some figuring to do. I'll be in my room."

"Listen to me for a minute, Maggie. This is—"

Brad stopped speaking when Janice nudged his leg with her toe under the table. Their eyes met as they listened to Maggie's footsteps hurrying up the stairs. "She hasn't walked that fast since Richie died," Janice said. She took the check from her husband's hand and tore it once and then again—and then again.

"She's going to make it," Janice said.

Ten days later, early, with the sun barely nudging the horizon, Maggie stood next to her dad's SUV with her father and mother. Cartoon balloons drifted from the mouths of each of them as they spoke, and a sharp, hostile wind stirred up dust devils and whisked the breath steam away.

Maggie studied her parents as they embraced one another, memories of her childhood flooding her mind, at least for short moments taking her back to an idyllic time when everything seemed perfect and peaceful and so wonderfully full of promise.

"Maggie?" Janice brought her daughter into the family embrace. The scent of the Clubman cologne on her father's freshly shaved face tickled Maggie's childhood memories once again—he'd used the product as long as she could remember. Janice's hair had a very light scent of lilacs, another sensory bit of her parents Maggie stored in her heart.

"Do me a favor today?" her father asked, his voice slightly muffled in Maggie's hair.

Maggie nodded, still embracing her parents, almost afraid to let go of them. "Sure . . . what?"

"Ride today, Maggie. Run the barrels, go out on a trail—but get on a horse."

"I will, Daddy. I promise."

The ground was flinty-hard that afternoon, but the persistent night wind had scoured the snow from the paddock. Maggie tugged her Stetson down at the brim, securing it against the sniping breeze. Happy was a good mare, a pretty fifteen-hand dappled gray with almost perfect legs. She was a fast and agile barrel horse, but, equally important, Happy was an endlessly willing mount with a heart bigger than the state of Montana.

Maggie shifted in her saddle, standing in the stirrups and then easing down onto Happy's back. She took a deep breath, and the familiar scents of Lexol saddle cleaner, sweet-feed breath, and the pure, clean aroma of cold horsehide enveloped her. The *chunk-chunk* of Happy's hooves hitting the ground was the only sound in the entire world, and that was just fine with Maggie. She eased the mare into a lope, following the three-railed fence and easing the corners of the rectangle into smooth left turns.

Maggie felt in control of this fine mount, if not in control of anything else in her life. She knew the feeling would last for only a mere speck of time—a quick shard that really changed nothing. But it felt good, at least momentarily.

She leaned forward slightly in the saddle and touched Happy's sides with her boot heels. Clumps of frozen soil pelted the air behind the mare as she hurled herself forward, scrambling to a full-out gallop within a few strides. Maggie rode with rather than on her mount, moving with the fluid, stunningly fast, controlled rampage. Her eyes streaming from the battering of the arctic air, Maggie touched Happy's mouth with a breath of rein pressure on the low port bit, easing her through a gentle turn to the left.

It wasn't until that moment that Maggie noticed the black GMC with Danny Pulver standing next to it in her driveway. Sunday, his copper and white coat gleaming in the harsh sunlight, stood next to Danny, apparently watching the barrel run as intently as his master.

The moment of solace Maggie had found in the saddle evaporated, leaving her once again empty. She raised a hand to Danny and hooked her horse in a turn to the far end of the paddock, away from the man and his dog. *A friend stops and I have to turn away from him so he can't see my face, the look that I know is there, the one that says "Leave me alone."*

Danny waited where he was until Maggie turned her mare and rode at a walk to the fence near him. "Good to see you, Maggie," he said.

"Good to see you too. C'mon into the barn while I put Happy up." Her eyes dropped to Sunday, whose tail was moving tentatively as he watched her. A genuine smile crossed her face as she met the big dog's eyes, much different than the one she'd forced to greet Danny.

"Hey, Sunday," she said. She'd met the collie a couple of times before, but only through the open window of the vet's truck. Still, even in those brief exchanges of ear scratching and hand sniffing, she'd felt a quick bond with the dog. He was a beautiful tawny creature, in vibrant good health, with a coat as polished as that of Lassie on the old TV show. That wasn't what attracted her to the collie, though. Sunday's eyes had reached into her own at those first meetings, just as they did now.

"OK if I let him explore?" Danny asked. "He won't get into anything."

"Sure, no problem. Come here, Sunday—say hello."

Danny snapped his fingers, and the dog rushed toward Maggie, tail swinging much harder now, his paws pattering over the frozen ground. As any male dog would, he skidded to a stop at the fence, sniffed a post, and swung his body to leave his signature scent.

"Does he know about . . ." Maggie began.

Sunday hefted a leg, and a stream of urine dashed against the fence post—as well as the resistor that held the smooth gray electrical wire that ran a foot off the ground around the entire paddock. The wire served a pair of purposes: it kept bored horses from toying with the fence, and it stunted or killed the weeds that grew along fence lines with its pulsing electricity. The power followed the liquid. Sunday was thrown back a yard by the assault, a yip punctuating his scrambling retreat. In the smallest part of a second, the eighty-pound collie turned into a warrior—and he attacked the post. This time, as his fangs slashed at the resistor, the wire pressed against his tongue and the jolt rolled him over in the dirt. His yowl of surprise and pain was almost puppylike as he got his feet under himself and stood glaring at the fence. A feral growl rumbled from his throat, the fur along his spine raised in challenge and his lips curled back, revealing snowy white eyeteeth.

Maggie turned away from the scene, her shoulders

shaking, laughing for the first time in what felt like forever. Danny, too, ducked his head and turned to his truck. The pulse of electricity was far too small to do a horse or Sunday any harm, but the collie's reaction—and the fact that he backed a full dozen feet away from the fence while issuing his challenge—was like an absurd pratfall from a silent movie. Even so, both Maggie and Danny realized that laughing out loud would hurt the animal's pride.

Danny, his face under strict control, walked to the gate and worked the latch, opening it for Maggie and her mare. Sunday waited until the gate was closed and Maggie and Happy were several steps toward the front door of the barn before he scurried up to her. She crouched and hugged the dog. "What a good, brave boy! You sure showed that fence, Sunday!"

Danny dropped to his knees next to Maggie, and Sunday turned to him. The vet rubbed his dog, hugged him, and then pointed away from the barn. "Good boy, Sunny—good dog. Go, now—go." The collie lapped Danny's hand and hustled off toward Maggie's house, knowing he was free to explore.

"He's magnificently trained," Maggie said.

"I wish I could claim credit for that, but I can't. Sun's a rare animal. I've had dogs—mostly collies—all my life, but he's . . . well . . . something else."

Maggie nodded and rose to her feet to bring Happy to her stall. "Yeah. The same thing happens with horses every so often. There are good ones and smart ones and willing ones—but then a really special horse comes along and captures a person's heart."

"Like Dancer?"

"Exactly." Maggie paused for a moment. "The same thing's true with people. The majority of us are good people who lead good lives, but we don't have that rare spark that some do."

"Like Rich?" Danny asked quietly.

"Yes. Like Rich." Her voice was barely a whisper.

"I didn't come up to you at church, Maggie, and I've stayed away until now because I didn't know what to say or how to say it. I still don't, I guess, but I didn't want to wait any longer."

Maggie began stripping Happy's saddle and saddle blanket off, looking over the mare's back at the vet.

"Rich was important to lots of us," Danny said. "I know what you mean about the rare people, the special people, and he was one of them. The thing is," he paused for a moment, searching for the right words, "I always felt good around him. He had a way of making a person feel better, somehow—more worthwhile, maybe. And there was no more prejudice to Rich Locke than there is to a newborn kitten. He was interested in each person he came across, wanted to know about them, what they thought, what they believed, how they lived. And that was real about him, Maggie. It wasn't hype or a façade—it was the way he was."

The barn was totally quiet for a long but not uncomfortable moment. The sun, ignoring the frigid temperature, streamed through the windows of the barn with mid-July clarity.

"Thanks, Dan," Maggie said. "What you said helps me."

"I want to do that. I want to help you all I can. I mean it, Maggie." Danny reached over Happy's back and touched Maggie's shoulder with his fingertips. Then, in a second, his face flushed and he withdrew his hand quickly. "I gotta go," he said. "I'll see you soon, OK? I just wanted to . . . I'll see you soon."

Maggie listened as the veterinarian whistled for Sunday, and then a moment later, to the grumble of his truck's engine as he drove the length of her driveway. She began roughing Happy's coat with a rubber curry comb, the familiar motions automatic. She was strangely unsettled by Dan Pulver's visit, and she wasn't at all sure why.

3

Maggie stood at her kitchen sink, running water over a cereal bowl. Outside her window the Montana sun played its duplicitous winter game: the light was exuberantly cheerful and the sky an impossible, welcoming blue, but the thermometer attached to the siding next to the window read four below zero.

She turned off the water and put the bowl and spoon in the drying rack. As she turned from the sink her eye caught a green spot on the shoulder of her work shirt. She looked closer. It was a strand of spittle—saliva mixed with bits of well-chewed hay—from Dusty's nudge of greeting that morning. "Yuck," she said aloud, reaching for a paper towel and cleaning away the deposit. Something ticked at the back of her mind as she tossed the paper towel into the trash can—something to do with the horses. She walked to the calendar tacked to the wall next to the telephone, but there was no entry made for the date. The horseshoer wasn't due, she didn't expect a hay delivery, and the supplement and sweet-feed barrels in the barn were full.

Maggie sighed. *Some days are better, some are worse. It's going to be a long haul. Time doesn't really cure all ills, but it diminishes the pain—makes it bearable for longer and longer periods of times. At first it was a frantic, screaming thing—knowing Richie was dead but not accepting it. But now some acclimation is beginning—I guess. Or maybe it's apathy. Maybe I just know my life is over.*

Maggie did her best to shrug the thought away. The task she'd promised herself that she'd complete this morning nagged at her like a toothache. She picked up the three large cardboard cartons she'd gotten at the grocery store the day before and started up the stairs, balancing the boxes in front of her. She stood staring into the closet she'd shared with Rich for a long moment, motionless, her mind rushing with confused, sharp-edged images.

Her mother, standing in the doorway of the bedroom, had to speak twice before Maggie really heard what she was saying. "Can I help you, honey? With two of us working, we'll finish in half the time."

"Thanks, Mom," Maggie said, turning to face her mother. "But I'd really like to do this alone. OK?"

"Sure, I understand. But if you need me, I'll be reading in my room."

Maggie turned back to the closet, willing herself to move yet remaining where she was. Rich's uniforms hung neatly on the left side of the walk-in closet—his side—in line with the one nonmilitary suit and couple of sport jackets he owned. There were perhaps seven or eight short- and long-sleeve shirts, a couple of ties, a few pairs of trousers on hangers, and a pair of scuffed and haggard-looking running shoes on the floor next to his Western boots.

I can do this, Maggie told herself as her lips moved silently to reinforce the thought.

And then she did. She worked rapidly but not sloppily, at times through a mist of tears. She folded the shirts into a box, covered them with some sweaters from the dresser, and then added rolled pairs of socks. Underwear, a thick leather belt with a large horse-head buckle, a handkerchief, and two more sweaters filled a second box. The uniforms Maggie left on the hangers, along with the sport jackets. The trousers, three pairs of jeans, two USAF sweatshirts, and the Western boots went into the third carton. That one was the most difficult to close. Maggie pictured a down-and-out guy at the Salvation Army getting a new start with Rich's things and then held on to that mental picture as long as she could as she sat on her bed and looked at the now seemingly cavernous closet.

Maggie stood from the bed, hefted two of the boxes, and carried them down the stairs. She stacked them in the living room just off the kitchen and went back upstairs for the third. Then she took Rich's roughout winter coat from the closet and placed it on top of the cartons.

The telephone call to the Salvation Army was easier than she thought it would be; they'd have a van to her place in the morning. The man who answered the phone at the Salvation Army service center recognized the Locke name. "We'll be right proud to share your husband's stuff with those who need it," he said. "Bless you, ma'am."

She was still holding the receiver after a mumbled thank-you when she heard a vehicle in her driveway. She stepped to the window and saw Danny Pulver's black GMC picking its way over the ruts toward the barn. A quick spark of irritation flushed her cheeks, and she was immediately aware of the fact that she no doubt smelled like a dockworker, that there was a sheen of sweat on her face from her efforts, and that she craved a shower infinitely more than she did a visitor. She pulled a sleeve across her forehead, retucked her shirt into her jeans, and went to the kitchen door.

"Danny," Maggie said. "Nice of you to stop by."

Danny had the slightly embarrassed look on his face that Maggie had come to recognize in the last few weeks, the "we both know your husband crashed his airplane into the ground and was killed, but let's not mention it" look.

The vet looked flustered for a moment. "Uh . . . I was scheduled to examine Dancer and Dusty today. If it's a bad time, I can come back in a few days. Or whenever."

"Oh, Danny—I'm sorry. I completely forgot the postnatal exams. Things have been so . . . Well, how about this—you go check the horses, and I'll make us a pot of coffee. Just come on in when you're finished."

"I don't want to cause you any trouble. I can check them over and be on my—"

"How much trouble is making coffee?"

A smile cut through the concern on Danny's face. "Great," he said.

"Is Sunday with you?" Maggie asked. "Will he remember the electric fence?"

Danny's grin broadened. "He'll never forget it—I'll guarantee that. He's in the truck."

"Why don't you let him out then. He's always welcome here—let him run."

"Thanks, Maggie. He's been in the truck most of the morning. He could use some exercise." Danny began to turn away and then stopped himself. "His tail started thumping as soon as I turned onto your road. You've got a new friend."

When Danny tapped on the back door forty-five minutes later, Janice Stuart let him in. "I'm Maggie's mother," she said. "Jan Stuart. Sit at the table, Dr. Pulver—Maggie's upstairs. She'll be down in a moment."

"Please, Mrs. Stuart, call me Danny."

"Only if you'll call me Jan."

The vet extended his hand, and Mrs. Stuart took it and they shook almost formally. "Hard times," Danny said. "I'm so sorry. I didn't know Rich terribly well, but I liked him a lot. I was there at the church but didn't get in the reception line. Maggie looked like she was ready to fall over."

Jan sighed at the memory. "As you said, Danny—hard times. For all of us."

Maggie's steps on the stairs put an end to the conversation. Danny stood in place and smiled at Maggie; suddenly he felt self-conscious.

"Sit, Mom, Danny," Maggie said. "The coffee should be ready in a minute. I put it on before I went to clean up."

Danny sat at the table and sniffed appreciatively. The

heady aroma of good-quality, strong, freshly brewed coffee was beginning to infuse the kitchen with its warmth.

"How are the patients, Danny?" Maggie asked, taking cups and saucers from the cabinet above the sink.

"Fit as can be. Dusty's fine—no pain on palpation, birth canal healing exactly as it should. She's a textbook mother. The problem with the umbilical cord was an anomaly—nothing more."

"And Dancer?"

"He's an amazing little guy—has a chest the size of a wine barrel already, and I've yet to come across a more curious foal. He couldn't be more healthy."

Jan, still standing, looked as if she'd been waiting for an opening. "No coffee for me just now, Maggie. I promised to call your dad this afternoon." She turned to Danny, who rose to take her hand once again. "Nice meeting you, Danny. Please come by again."

"Same here, Jan. I'll do that."

Jan's exit left an uncomfortable void. Danny sensed that Maggie was also aware that the last time they'd been together in this room, Rich had been with them.

Danny cleared his throat as Maggie brought the coffeepot from the stove and filled their cups. "I saw your ad in *Horse Trader*, Maggie. You're selling most of your stock?"

Maggie sat across from the vet. "It's not what I want to do, but I have no choice. I can earn more training horses for barrel racing and cutting horse events and giving lessons to riders, and there's almost no overhead on that other than my time. I like the breeding aspect of it, but for now

I've got to cut back. If I can stay here, maybe later on I'll be able to—"

"You're moving away?" Danny's words came a bit too quickly.

"No—at least I hope not," Maggie said. "But I have a few financial . . . difficulties. It's nothing I can't handle, but it's tight just now. I'm planning to breed Dusty and two of the mares I'm keeping, and I'll be campaigning Dancer if he lives up to what he shows now."

"He will. You can bet on it."

Her smile looked forced. "That's pretty much what I'm doing." She paused. "If I have to, I'll sell the six or eight acres of timber on the west line of our place. I don't want to, but it may come to that."

Danny nodded.

Maggie stood and stepped to her purse on the counter near the stove, taking out her checkbook. "Before I forget, what do I owe you for today?"

"Look, Maggie . . ."

"Don't start that nonsense with me. I'm not a starving widow, and I pay my bills. You have to make a living just like everyone else." Her tone wasn't exactly heated, but it wasn't far from that, either.

"Whoa!" Danny said. "That isn't what I meant at all. I was thinking of a barter. I've been looking for a riding horse—a gelding or mare I can poke around trails on. A pleasure horse, really. Sunday and I both need the exercise."

"Good for you. But I don't know what you mean about a barter."

"Well, the thing is, I know the anatomy and I can pick out a good, healthy horse with no major flaws or physical problems. It's temperament I'm concerned about, and I don't know anyone more skilled at reading a horse than you. I thought that when I find one I like, I'd ask you to spend an hour or so on him—or her. I just want to hack around on horseback, but I don't want to spend money on a horse that's silly or lazy or has bad habits. See what I mean?"

Maggie sat again and sipped at her coffee. "With some horses I could tell you what you want to know in twenty minutes, Danny. With others I'd need some time—at least a full day, maybe a couple of days."

"OK. I'll pay you for your time by doing routine stuff on your horses."

"And I'll pay you for yours by checking out horses for you? That could work. But not for today's fee. What do I owe you?"

It was Danny's turn to drink from his cup to buy a moment of time. "Fair enough. The barn call is thirty-five, and the exams—"

"Don't get cute, Danny," Maggie said, but this time with the beginning of a real smile. "I know your barn call fee is forty-five."

Danny shrugged, feeling the heat of embarrassment coloring his face. "OK—the total is seventy dollars."

Maggie opened her checkbook, placed it on the counter, and took a ballpoint from her purse. She wrote and signed the check and met Danny's eyes. "No more games—please.

This is business. Anything beyond exams I'll pay the same that any of your customers do. Agreed?"

Danny accepted the check, folded it in half, and slid it into the pocket of his blue work shirt. "Agreed."

That night, Maggie turned on the light on her bedside table after almost two hours of seeking sleep that consistently and cruelly eluded her. She pushed back the now-twisted sheets and blankets and sat up, feet on the floor, shoulders slumped, hands in her lap. Her clock radio glowed 2:47 as if it were mocking her. Her eyes focused on her Bible on the shelf of her bedside table. She leaned forward to pick it up, and the worn leather cover felt gritty under her fingertips. She hadn't held the book since Christmas Eve, when she and Rich had taken turns reading from Luke, as they'd done faithfully each December 24 of their married life.

She set the book on her lap and gently brushed the dust from its cover. *I'm empty. Where there's supposed to be feeling there's none—it's exactly as if all life and love have been plucked out of me and I'm a husk that moves around and pretends it's alive but isn't. And I'm alone. Even with my mother in the next room, I'm alone.*

A concept—an image—that Rev. Traynor had used in a sermon a couple of years ago flitted into her mind. He'd said, "I have no idea where or when I read this, but it's one of my very favorite concepts. Imagine if the moon were made of the hardest substance known to mankind—that it was the same size as it is now, but instead of dust and rubble, it was a gigantic, impossibly huge diamond. Now, imagine a little dove. Watch in your mind as the dove begins a flight to the moon and after countless years reaches it. As she passes by she gently touches one of her wings to the diamond moon and then flies back to earth, where she begins the trip all over again." The reverend waited for a long moment. Then, he said, "When that grand, gigantic diamond is gone, rubbed away to nothingness by the sweet touch of the dove's wing, eternity will barely have begun."

Maggie choked then, and the Bible thumped to the floor in front of her, between her bare feet. *That's how long I'll feel like this, and that's how long I'll love Richie.* Tears came then and stayed with her until the soft pastels of dawn began to play in the eastern sky.

Taking care of animals didn't allow Maggie a lot of time for grief, and her domesticated horses required more hours and effort than most large animals except perhaps dairy cattle. There was feeding to be done twice daily, stalls to be mucked out, fresh straw to be spread, and well-trained, high-maintenance barrel-racing horses to be exercised at least three times per week.

Maggie did what she had to do, and it filled some of the hollow places in her days. The work was essentially mindless: lift, carry, rake, shovel—and there was no joy to it. At one time Maggie had reveled in the scents of the barn and the personalities of her horses. Their need for attention and affection had touched her, and the carrots and half apples she offered the horses on a flattened palm were gifts of love. Those benefits—the sweaty pleasures of working with the animals—seemed to have drifted off into the sky with the smoke from Rich's X-417.

She slumped down, sitting on a bale of hay outside a stall, and let her pitchfork drop from her fingers. *If we'd had a child, there'd be something left of Rich other than pain and longing.* A vision of a toddler in tiny jeans and Western boots and a shirt with little pearl snaps appeared in her mind. Maggie saw herself holding out her arms to her baby, but when the baby turned, the face was Rich's.

She stood quickly, angrily, and snatched her manure fork from the floor on her way up. *I can't do this. I won't do this—I won't let myself slip into becoming a delusional, whining widow. I won't be a crazy lady sitting in a corner, twisting a Kleenex to bits and feeling sorry for myself. I always knew that flying those things was a gamble, a roll of the dice, every time he went up.* She eased herself down to the cement floor of the barn again, this time on her knees, and set her pitchfork aside.

But, Lord, it's so hard . . .

The prayer stopped there. She had no words, no images, nothing to convey except her bleakness and despair. This time, not even tears would come.

Maggie had both anticipated and dreaded the day her mother left. Forcing smiles and rehearsing chitchat were heavy and unnatural burdens for Maggie, but when her mother was gone, her love and her very presence were deeply missed.

Six weeks had passed since Maggie had driven Janice to the airport, and the following days had blended into one another, like spilled paint of different colors taking on a drab sameness, a dull monotony.

Maggie stood outside Dusty and Dancer's stall with Dr. Pulver, marveling, even through the lethargy that had become as much a part of her life as breathing, at the rate of growth of the colt. His legs, still spindly, seemed ludicrously long for the size of his body. But his hips were filling out, beginning to take on the breadth of the quarter horse butt—the powerful launching pad that provided the breed with its lightning acceleration. Danny reached out and scratched Dancer between the ears. The colt grunted with pleasure.

His head and muzzle had grown too—Dancer no longer had the deerlike quality of a very young horse. His eyes, liquid, shiny, and insistently curious, drew the gaze of anyone who looked at him. And Dusty's grooming, her constant licking and nuzzling, kept her foal's coat show-ring perfect.

"I'd start putting them out a couple of hours a day," Danny said, palming an apple to Dusty. "Mama's going to go nuts in here if she doesn't get some exercise." He leaned over the top rail of the stall. "She hasn't missed many meals, has she? Some of that's postpartum, but she's starting to look like a bowl of Jell-O."

"She'll work it off when Dancer's weaned," Maggie said.

"She's a good mother, isn't she?" It wasn't actually a question; she knew Danny knew the answer.

"The best. Look at Dancer's coat—not a manure stain or a bit of straw clinging to him." Danny focused on the colt for a moment. "He's going to be tall. I wouldn't doubt that he goes over sixteen hands as a two-year-old. He'll be rangy too. His bones are long."

Dancer, catching the scent of the apple his mother was industriously chewing, moved to her head and reached upward to her mouth. Then the colt amazed both Maggie and Danny: he shifted his body, rose quickly and gracefully upward, and placed his forefeet on Dusty's neck, his muzzle probing at her mouth, seeking the apple.

"Whew," Danny breathed. "This boy is agile! I've never seen one this young use his body and balance like that. Never."

Dusty quickly had enough of her son prodding his muzzle at her mouth and shook her head and neck. Dancer settled back on all fours—and took a quick nip at her side. Dusty spun toward him, spewing bits of partially chewed apple, and bared her teeth at the colt. Dancer backed rapidly into a corner of the stall, shrinking somehow, his stance and his eyes frightened. Dusty glared at him for a long moment and then turned away, snorting sharply to show her anger.

"Attagirl, Dusty!" Danny laughed. "Don't let that rabbit chew holes in your hide."

A gust of wind rattled a window, and Dancer, still in the corner, focused his attention on the sound, his ear tips pointing toward it. The sounds of the barn—the occasional creak of wood, the light buffeting of the wind against the outside, Dusty's now slower and rhythmic grinding of the apple—were comfortable ones, sounds both Danny and Maggie had enjoyed for years, without really paying a great deal of attention to them. Perhaps it was the breaking of that peace that made them more embarrassed than they should have been when they both began to speak at once.

"No—go on, Danny," Maggie said.

"I was just saying that we haven't seen you in church for a lot of weeks. You're missed, Maggie. Ellie asked about you."

"I've been busy. People wanting to check out horses to buy want to do it on weekends, and that includes Sundays."

"Sure," Danny said. "That's true." After a moment, he said, "How about if I stop by tomorrow and kind of watch things and you go to church? If anyone shows up to look at a horse, I'll say you'll be back in a bit, and they'll wait if they're interested enough."

Maggie shook her head. "No—no thanks, Danny." That the words came abruptly wasn't lost on either of them.

Maggie saw that her fingers were clenched so tightly on the top board of the stall that her knuckles were a pale white. She squeezed her eyes shut as a blockade against the tears that were already flowing. Danny reached his arms out to her, and she stepped quickly into his hug, pressing her face against his chest, rocking both their bodies with her wrenching sobs.

The sound of a car outside separated them. Maggie used her hands to wipe tears from her face, and her eyes found a wet spot the size of a saucer on Danny's shirt. "I'm sorry," she said, trying for a smile she didn't feel. "I cried all over your shirt."

Danny grinned. "That's not nearly as bad as what a German shepherd pup did on the first shirt I put on this morning."

An auto horn, deep and resonant, sounded from outside. Maggie rushed to the faucet used to fill water buckets and ran the icy cold water on her hands, and then rubbed her face. "Somebody to see a horse, I guess," she said. "I need to . . ."

"Yeah," Danny said quickly. "I gotta shove off."

"We'll talk soon, OK?"

"Sure, Maggie. Let's do that."

Maggie hustled past him to the front of the barn and stepped out into the sunlight. A metallic blue Rolls-Royce sedan idled smoothly on the concrete apron, the sun sending shards of light from the highly polished automobile that were almost painful to Maggie's eyes. The driver's door swung open as Danny left the barn and walked toward his GMC, openly eyeing the expensive British luxury vehicle. He grinned when he saw the two people in the car.

"Hi, Dr. Morrison, Tessa. Sorry, I've got to run."

Both women in the car waved to the vet. "Ms. Locke?" the older woman asked, easing out of the car. There was an understated elegance to her that was impossible to miss. Her face was richly tanned, and Maggie could tell that the tan came from the sun, not from a series of carcinogenic light tubes. The woman's charcoal slacks were simple and perfectly cut, and her white silk blouse and light jacket didn't come from Target, where Maggie shopped. There were no rings on her fingers; she wore small gold studs in her ears but no other jewelry. It was her face, though, that transfixed Maggie. She wasn't beautiful by contemporary standards—she had an actual woman's form rather than the stick-figure physique of fashion models—but the high, softly defined cheekbones and the liquid depth of her cornflower-blue eyes were striking. The word *patrician* flitted into Maggie's mind.

"I'm Sarah Morrison," the woman said as she walked toward Maggie and extended her hand. Her voice was a bit deeper than Maggie expected, with a texture of the South to it. Maggie wiped her right palm on her jeans and took the offered hand.

"Maggie Locke, Ms. Morrison. Pleased to meet you."

"Sarah suits me better. May I call you Maggie?"

"Of course."

Sarah was older than Maggie had initially estimated—perhaps well into her fifties. Her age detracted not in the least from her presence and the aura of gentility that she projected.

"We spoke very briefly early last week. About the horse for my daughter." The passenger door of the Rolls opened, and a smaller, much younger version of Sarah Morrison got out of the car and looked over at the two women. She was about fourteen and was dressed in well-worn jeans, a Western shirt, scuffed but clean boots, and an unbuttoned, lined Levi jacket. Her eyes, Maggie realized even with the distance between them, were precise reproductions of her mother's—except that the girl's were sparkling with excitement and anticipation.

"My daughter, Tessa," Sarah said.

The girl moved forward, a tentative smile showing a few thousand dollars' worth of silver braces on her teeth. She was thin-limbed and coltish as she walked to Maggie with her left hand extended. It was then Maggie noticed that the child's right sleeve was empty and hanging vacantly at her side. Maggie put out her left hand to the girl, pleased that the motion had been smooth, without fumbling or confusion.

"I lost it a long time ago," Tessa said, answering the unasked question. "No big deal. I hold the reins in my left hand—as I'm supposed to—when I'm trail riding. When I run barrels I use a game rein—a single piece. As I said, it's no big deal."

"Glad to meet you, Tessa," Maggie said. *How many kids today know the difference between* like *and* as*—and use the words correctly?*

"When we spoke, you mentioned a horse named Tinker," Sarah said. "A five-year-old mare?"

Maggie looked at Tessa. "I'm awfully sorry, but Tinker's been sold."

Tessa swallowed hard, and her eyes lost their sparkle. "I see," she said. "I wish we could have come sooner. Dr. Pulver said good things about Tinker. I already knew that you and Tinker won open barrel racing at Tri-County last summer."

"I'm sorry, honey," Sarah said, stepping to her daughter and touching her face gently. She looked at Maggie. "I'm a cardiac surgeon, and my schedule has been horrendous—one emergency after another. I should've had our groundskeeper bring Tessa over to look at the mare, but I wanted to see Tinker too."

Maggie had learned to live with the slight swelling she'd felt in her throat since she'd stood in the same barnyard and heard Rich's plane strike the earth. The lump she felt now was different—maybe because she could do something about this one.

"How good are you, Tessa? Really—no hype. Tell me when you started and tell me what you've done on horseback."

Much of the life came back to the girl's eyes. "I'll be fourteen in a couple of months."

"Six," Sarah noted. "Six months."

"And I've had weekly lessons since I was about eight. My dad wanted me to ride a pancake, but I told him I wouldn't ride a saddle without a horn. I've been to horse camps each summer."

"How were the camps?" Maggie asked.

"Not good—but I got to ride a whole lot. I didn't go to learn about rock stars, makeup, and boys. I wanted to learn to ride Western horses and to run barrels."

Maggie's smile came quickly and naturally, and it felt slightly strange on her face, as if those muscles hadn't been used much in the past months. "What are the main bone structures in a horse's legs, Tessa?" she asked.

There was no pause for thought before the girl answered. "Cannon, fetlock, and pastern."

"OK." Maggie laughed. "How about this: what do Arabian horses have that other breeds don't?"

"Two things—an extra vertebra and a third eyelid, a membrane that protects their eyes in sandstorms."

"Very good, Tessa—you've done your reading. That's important."

The young girl's smile was the first burst of radiant sunshine following a long day of drizzle and clouds. "Thanks, Mrs. Locke."

"Call me Maggie." She thought for a moment. "I have a five-year-old quarter horse gelding named Turnip who knows the barrel pattern but tends to be a little silly at times—and he's headstrong too. There's not a mean bone in Turnip's body, but he'll take advantage of a rider if he's allowed to do so."

She met Tessa's eyes. "One thing—if you've been riding school horses and camp stock, you've probably never ridden a horse with the speed this guy has. He's a fireball, and he needs good, confident hands on the reins."

"A good, confident *hand* on the reins," Tessa corrected.

Maggie's move was totally spontaneous, as was the heat she felt in her eyes, as she put her arms out to the girl and Tessa moved to her hug. The contact with another body, the sensation of the child's arm around her, the faint, sweet scent of bubble gum and shampoo and the deeper animal smell of horse on Tessa's Levi jacket were almost too much for Maggie to bear. She stepped back from the girl. "I'm sorry . . ."

"We know about your husband, Maggie," Sarah said quietly. "Ellie Traynor has been friends with my folks back in Boston forever. I always called her Aunt Ellie, and I still do. Tessa and I moved here from Boston a few weeks ago. Aunt Ellie told us about you."

"She also told us that you have the best quarter horses in the world," Tessa added.

"Actually, she said the best in Montana," Sarah said.

Maggie stepped back and wiped the tears from her cheeks with the backs of her hands. "Turnip is in the third stall on the left," she said. "There's a good Western saddle on a sawhorse just inside the barn—you can use that. How about if you tack up Turnip and bring him out here? His bridle and bit are hanging on his stall door." She turned to Sarah suddenly. "Oh—Sarah. I'm sorry. I mean, if it's OK with you that Tessa takes a look at the horse. I could go in and get him, if you like."

Tessa looked imploringly at her mother, then at Maggie. "I brought my own saddle. It's a Martha Josie model—made for running barrels. Is it OK if I use that?"

"Go on," Maggie said. Tessa wasted no time hustling into the barn. "What a wonderful girl. She's precious, Sarah."

"I won't argue with you on that point. She was ten when she lost her arm in Kenya, on a safari with her father. We're divorced. He's a surgeon too. Tessa was bitten by some sort of bizarre insect, and gangrene set in and the doctors there had no choice. The thing is, she never said a thing to her dad about her arm. She wore long-sleeved shirts, and he never noticed it until it was too late to save it. She didn't want to ruin the safari for him." Her voice broke slightly in her final sentence. "That's the type of kid she's always been."

"You must be very proud."

"I am, but I'm also concerned that my daughter may be suffering because so much of my time is spent elbow-deep in someone's chest." Sarah took a deep breath. "That's a big part of why I agreed to buy a horse for her. There are so many traps for teens with too much time and not enough to do. She loves horses, Maggie. I think having her own to be responsible for would be good for her."

Maggie nodded. "When I look at Tessa I see myself at her age, horse crazy and very happy, with dirt under my fingernails and calluses on my hands from shoveling manure and tossing bales of hay. It's a great way to grow up."

The sharp ring of steel horseshoes on cement drew the attention of both women from their conversation. Tessa led the saddled and bridled Turnip from the barn, walking on his right side, reins in her left hand.

Turnip gawked at the unfamiliar Rolls-Royce, snorted, and stopped when Tessa did, his muzzle a foot or so behind her head. He stood 15.2 hands, a hand being four inches and the standard equine height measurement, gauged from the withers to the ground. His coat was a light butterscotch color—buckskin—and his tail and mane were darker, approaching black. His chest, broad and hard, flowed to strong, tightly muscled legs and decent-sized hooves. His ears, perked like those of a curious fox, flicked from Tessa to

Maggie, and then back to Tessa. His back was straight, and his withers not prominent but well formed. His rear end was wide and smooth, and he shagged an imaginary fly with his tail, as if showing off its length and thickness.

"Wow," Sarah said.

"Yeah," Maggie agreed. "Isn't he the prettiest thing you've ever seen? He knows it too—look at him preening like a prom queen."

Tessa led the gelding closer to the women. The girl's eyes told far more than her words could convey. She'd fallen deeply in love with the handsome and arrogant animal, and she completely believed that he was the finest, noblest, most perfect horse in the world. "Where'd he get the name Turnip?" she asked, then quickly added, looking into the horse's eyes, "Not that I don't like the name, of course."

"Nothing too romantic about it, I'm afraid," Maggie said. "A neighbor dropped off a little basket of turnips from her garden when he was a foal. I gave him a small one, and he loved it. We even did a comparison test—let him have his choice between a piece of turnip and a piece of apple. He always went for the turnip first. The name just stuck." She turned to Tessa's mother. "Sarah?" Maggie asked. "Can Tessa try him out in the arena? Poke around on him a little, get a feel for him?"

Sarah laughed. "It's either that or have my daughter disown me, I guess."

Maggie walked toward the gate to the arena, Tessa and Turnip slightly behind her. "He hasn't been out in a couple of days, and he'll be a little antsy. He'll probably do some crow-hopping. Can you ride to that?"

Tessa grinned. "Like a burr on a saddle blanket."

Maggie swung the gate open, and Tessa led Turnip inside and stepped easily into the saddle, reins held loosely. She centered her weight on the horse and clucked him into a walk. Turnip took a few strides, snuffed, shook his head, and tried to skitter into a faster gait. Tessa's left hand moved almost imperceptibly on the reins, barely touching the low port bit in the horse's mouth. He snuffed again and danced sideways, arguing with his rider, testing her. Tessa gathered him in and again started him forward at a walk. Turnip, frustrated, launched his body off the ground, arching his back, and landed heavily on all four hooves.

"That's crow-hopping," Maggie said to Sarah. Sarah didn't answer. She stood transfixed, hand to her mouth, as if her daughter were walking on a tightrope above a vast chasm. "Relax," Maggie added. "Tessa knows what she's doing."

Turnip jumped again, this time more closely approximating a bronc-type buck. Tessa reined his head to the left and forced him to walk in a tight circle, his nose pointed at his tail. After a pair of revolutions Tessa straightened him again and applied some leg pressure, putting him into a jog. His action was initially stiff but quickly smoothed to the lazy-looking fluidity of a pace he could maintain for miles without tiring.

Tessa used the entire arena, following the fence, and her turns at the corners were wide sweeps. The young girl rode confidently, naturally, without the quick, jerky movements of legs and body that indicated someone new to the sport.

"She's very good, Sarah."

Tessa's mother had relaxed considerably. Her hand was no longer at her mouth, and a proud smile brightened her face. "They look . . . what? . . . natural together, don't they? Like they're partners somehow."

Maggie waved, caught Tessa's eye, and held up three fingers—the judge's sign in a Western show for riders in the ring to lope their horses. Tessa nodded and clucked at Turnip. He responded in a half heartbeat, flowing into an extended gait, several notches down from a gallop. Tessa guided her mount through broad, almost geometrically precise figure eights, using most of the arena. Turnip changed leads at the center each time. When he faltered Tessa used a slight shift in her body weight to guide him into taking the proper lead. The girl's face was a study in innocent, totally articulated joy.

"Can you keep him here until I can get a stable built? I'll pay whatever the boarding fee is, of course," Sarah said. "And I was wondering . . . are you working with students? I know that you did before Rich's accident. If it's too soon, I completely understand."

Maggie waved Tessa in and began to open the gate. "If you hadn't mentioned it," she said with a smile that actually felt real to her, "I'd have insisted that it be part of the deal."

Tessa dismounted inside the arena, her eyes riveted to her mother's face.

"He's all yours, honey," Sarah called to her daughter. "Turnip is your horse."

4

The August sun hung in the Montana sky like an immense bronze disk, already exerting its stultifying power and drawing the overnight dew from the pastures of Maggie's ranch the way a parched sea sponge draws water: greedily, hungrily. There was no breeze, and the air, at barely 7:00 in the morning, was already sultry and weighty with humidity. The sky, a deep cobalt, completely cloudless, held the oppressive heat between itself and the earth like a cosmic blanket. The early couple of hours were the best to trail ride. The heat wouldn't yet drain horse or rider, and the clouds of insects that plagued both animals and humans weren't quite ready to begin their day of buzzing harassment.

Sunday pushed his muzzle against Maggie's leg as she stood at the fence line closest to her house, watching Dusty and Dancer in the pasture. Dusty was cropping grass, her tail in almost constant motion while shagging flies. Dusty seemed completely at peace, but Maggie noticed that the mare's eyes never, not for the briefest part of a second, left her son as he played nearby.

Dancer, at least in his own mind, was engaged in a duel to the death with an invisible foe. The colt ran the center of the pasture at a full-steam gallop, neck extended, forelegs reaching ahead of him, deer-sized hooves glinting with dew as he raced through the grass, a mere inch ahead of the terrible enemy who pursued him. His body, still appearing angular and foal-like, was incompatible with his speed. Such foolishly sticklike legs simply couldn't move in that unfailing precision, and his narrow chest couldn't possibly process enough air for such a headlong run. Nevertheless, Dancer coursed across the pasture with the grace of a greyhound, the *thok* of his hooves against the dirt metronomic, an unvarying cadence.

When Dancer suddenly turned to face his awesome foe, Maggie drew a sharp breath of surprise. The colt dropped his rump almost to the ground, skidding on his rear hooves, front legs extended, and then wheeled his body back over his haunches in a training-text perfect maneuver called a "rollback" by Western riders. In a speck of time, Dancer was up on his hind legs, teeth bared, front hooves striking out again and again, battering and slashing his adversary. When the creature was dead on the grass, Dancer trotted back to his mother, head high.

Maggie shook her head in awe. Sunday bumped her harder. She turned to him and crouched down, eyes at the level of the dog's. "What do you need, Sunny? Is your water dish empty? Little jealous of Danny spending so much time with that new horse?"

The vet's nine-year-old Appaloosa gelding had been

boarding in Maggie's barn since Maggie had spent a day with Danny checking out the horse. Dakota, a rangy, quiet mount, was perfect for Danny—the gelding had enough speed to satisfy the vet during the rare times he galloped but was tractable enough to put up with the mistakes of relatively new riders. Dakota's trail manners were superb, and he was a willing animal with the friendly and open disposition that was standard in good Appaloosas.

Maggie walked toward the kitchen door, Sunday at her side. The economy-sized box of Milk-Bones she'd bought for Sunday on her last shopping trip was on the counter inside, within easy reach without tracking dirt or manure into the kitchen. She grabbed a pair of the biscuits from the box, dug a little deeper, and found a broken piece as well. Sunday sat as he'd been trained to do, awaiting his treat, his plumed tail sweeping the ground behind him. Maggie tossed the broken piece, and the dog snatched it out of the air, his teeth clacking together with a disconcertingly powerful snap.

Danny, Maggie realized, wouldn't own anything but a perfectly trained and mannerly dog. She knew that she could put a biscuit on the ground, tell Sunday no, and walk away, completely sure that the Milk-Bone would be untouched hours later. But there was much more to Sunday than his training. He was an honest dog—an animal totally without duplicity or guile. His heart was as big as all of Montana, and when he chose a human to be a friend, he'd gladly offer his life for that person's happiness.

Maggie stooped over to pet Sunday and heaved a sigh. For

no real reason it had been a particularly bad day for Maggie. She'd struggled to keep her mask in place until Danny had saddled Dakota and ridden off with Tessa to explore the trails, the two of them jabbering together about the wonders of their respective horses. When their voices and the hoofbeats had died out, Maggie had collapsed onto a bale of hay with her back against the barn wall. Sunday, whining softly deep in his throat, poked his elegant muzzle at his friend's face, licking away her tears and pushing against her legs with his body. Somehow the eighty-pound dog had climbed into her lap, his paws on her shoulders and his head tight to hers, his whining now constant and louder, sharing every iota of her loss and her misery. Maggie had hugged the dog that morning as she hadn't hugged anyone since Rich's death, and had felt the texture of Sunday's coarse Scottish coat and the scent of pasture grass envelop her.

Maggie knew that to an outsider, the image would have been ludicrous—an upset, red-faced woman with a dog that didn't weigh much less than she did clumsily situated in her lap. She also knew that Sunday's love was better medicine than any pharmacist in any drugstore could possibly offer.

The ringing of the telephone brought Maggie out of her reverie. She tossed a Milk-Bone to Sunday and hurried into the kitchen. The phone had startled her; it hadn't been ringing much lately. She'd sold the horses she needed to sell, keeping only Happy, Dusty, and Dancer. Rebel, a barrel-racing gelding she'd been training for over two years, had gone to a sister barrel racer who made a cash offer

Maggie found impossible to refuse, although she hated to part with the horse.

Ellie Traynor's voice was immediately identifiable, her warmth and caring almost as apparent over fiber-optic lines as they were in person. "It's good to hear your voice," Ellie said. "It's been way too long, honey, and that's my fault. But so much has been going on here. How are you doing?"

Maggie paused for a moment and then gave her practiced response. "I'm OK. A day at a time, you know? But I'm doing fine."

"Sure you are, Maggie—just like I'm entering steer wrestling at your next rodeo."

"Ellie . . ."

"No, honey, don't 'Ellie' me. I need you to stop by this morning. It's important." There'd been a not-so-subtle shift in Ellie's voice. She rarely gave orders or made personal demands on her friends or members of her husband's congregation, but this was both, and Maggie realized that.

"Do I need to change clothes? Otherwise I can leave immediately."

"Heavens no—come on ahead. I'll put on some of that English breakfast tea you like right now."

Maggie's four-year-old Chevy pickup coughed a bit when she first started it, but after a few moments, the idle settled down and the big V-8 rumbled smoothly. She glanced at the odometer. Eighty-eight thousand miles, a good part of it hard duty hauling a horse and trailer. *'Bout time for a tune-up.* She smirked. *Not with seventeen dollars in my checking account, though. The work can wait for a bit—it'll have to.*

Helmut and Ellie Traynor's home looked exactly like what a pastor and his wife's home should look like: small, neat, welcoming, with well-tended flower boxes on the front porch and a small but closely mown and healthy lawn on either side of the freshly swept sidewalk. The cottage was like Ellie herself, aging gracefully but showing the years and proud of them, still strong and able to nurture and protect anyone in need of shelter and warmth, be it from the elements or from physical or emotional pain.

Ellie opened the door before Maggie could use the little brass knocker, and the women embraced. "Come in, come in," Ellie said, smiling. "Let's go to the kitchen. The tea's ready and waiting."

Sunlight poured into the small kitchen through immaculate windows with homemade gingham curtains. "This is such a delightful room," Maggie said. "If Norman Rockwell were to paint the kitchen that everyone had or wished they had during their childhood, this would be the one he'd use for a model."

The older woman smiled. "When we moved in, there was an icebox—and we had ice delivered twice a week. There was a hand pump in the sink, and during the driest summers I built up my arm muscles flailing the handle to draw up enough water to do dishes." She looked around herself. "I think I like the electric refrigerator and water pump much better. Still, the old memories are good to have."

Ellie poured tea from a ceramic pot into the two cups she'd already placed in saucers on the table. Maggie watched her friend's hands, aware of the brown liver spots and the almost imperceptible tremble she'd never noticed before.

Ellie sat down across from the younger woman and sipped her tea. "How're you doing, Maggie? Will you talk with me? Can I share your hardship with you?"

Maggie twisted the paper napkin from beside her cup into a knot on her lap, her palms suddenly damp. "Soon, I think, but not just now, Ellie. I'm moving ahead most days—I really am—but . . . well . . ."

Ellie sighed. "One thing I've learned through all my years as a minister's wife is patience, Maggie. I've learned it—but I'm still not very good at it. I've prayed for you and about you every day since Rich died. In my arrogance, I questioned the Lord—badgered him, actually—demanding that he put his hand on your shoulder, give you the relief that you need, hold you in his warmth."

"Ellie . . ."

The elderly woman held up her hand, asking Maggie to wait. "That isn't the way it's done, honey. None of us as children of God have the right or the power to tell him how to run things." She sighed again. "As I prayed last night, the Lord pushed me back into line, sort of. He told me that Maggie Locke is his daughter—his beloved child—and that he will do what is best for her, in his time and in his way." She smiled then, and her eyes held with Maggie's. "What he said, in essence, was this: 'Look here, achy old woman who can remember her kindergarten teacher's name but can't recall if she took her medication five minutes ago, I'll tend to my Maggie. I have grand and joyous plans for her.

I haven't forgotten her, and I won't forget her. Accept that, OK? Because frankly, you're driving me batty with your mandates and imperatives. You haven't doubted me before, old woman. Don't doubt me in this.'" Ellie reached across the table to touch Maggie's face. "Are we together here?"

"It's not you, Ellie," Maggie protested. "It's . . . everything. Everything reminds me of him, and I dream of him fighting that airplane and calling out to me, and there isn't another person in the world who understands that—the stupid, bitter helplessness and the loneliness." Her words came in a hurried slew of emotion.

"Maggie," Ellie said quietly, "I miss Helmut every day, just as you miss Richie. But I haven't been alone since we buried Helmut. For a time, I thought I was—I felt as you do now. But I was wrong. The Lord was with me, just as he's with you. He is with you, honey . . ."

Maggie felt the sun on the back of her neck from the window behind her, and the sensation confused her for a moment. She'd been somewhere inside Ellie's words—a place where there was peace and faith in God and life was full and just and joyous.

Ellie sat back. "I'm leaving Coldwater, honey. I have Alzheimer's and arthritis, and my heart's failing, and I have to wrap my legs with stretch bandages every morning so I can stand up, and I'm tired. I'm going to Michigan to be with my sister. I'll read books and drink tea and sleep in the morning and be a little old lady waiting for the Lord. But Maggie—you'll remain in my heart and in my prayers. You must know that, and you must believe that."

"I do—but your friends, Ellie. You can't go away. You can't leave us." Maggie stopped to draw breath, and her heart clenched like a strong fist in her chest. "No—I mean . . . what I'm saying is . . . what about me, Ellie? I haven't been able to confide in you yet, but I've always known you were here. Now . . ."

"Hush for a moment, Maggie. The search committee has found a real man of God. A minister who'll fit here, a minister who believes what the Book says, and lives by it. His name is Ian Lane."

"He won't be Helmut, Ellie, and he won't be you. Couldn't you stay on and maybe cut back on what you do? It won't be at all the same if you leave Coldwater. Everyone in the church, everyone in the town—"

"No," Ellie interrupted, "and it shouldn't be the same, Maggie—I'm ill and I'm old and everything has changed around me and I've remained the same, and now my memory is shot and my body is telling me to go out and shop for a shroud while I still know what the word means. I want this, honey—I want to be with my sister, where all I'll have to plan ahead is whether we'll have toasted cheese sandwiches or tuna salad for lunch, and my biggest problem will be whether I've fed Monica's cats too much."

"How bad is the Alzheimer's, Ellie? How sick are you?"

Ellie stared off into space for a long moment, as if adding a long list of numbers in her mind. "You seem like a nice young lady," she finally said. "I'm pleased to meet you. What's your name?"

Maggie choked on her tea. "Stop that!" she demanded. "Your mind is sharper than a . . ."

"Than a marshmallow," Ellie finished for her. "Here's the prognosis, Maggie: I'm losing things, blocks of memory, daily. I have some sort of cardiac problem that makes my heart pound like a trip hammer, and that isn't at all good at my age. And I'm tired, honey. Ian's good—and he's smart too—and he's actually funny, which is an attribute so many young ministers don't have. Promise me you'll talk with him."

"I don't know. I still need some time. Can you accept that?"

"I can. Ian won't be here for another six weeks. You can let him settle in a bit—a couple of weeks at the outside—and then call and make an appointment with him. Agreed, Maggie?"

Maggie nodded, again meeting Ellie's eyes. "OK."

"One other thing, honey," Ellie said. "Are you aware that Danny Pulver is in love with you? And that he probably has been since before Richie died?"

Maggie shifted gears and steered her truck mechanically, barely aware of what she was doing. The smoky flavor of Ellie's tea was unpleasant in her mouth, harsh and metallic. The natural summertime beauty of Montana was lost on her, the richness of colors and textures not only unappreciated but unseen.

"Are you aware that Danny Pulver is in love with you?"

Ellie's words played in Maggie's mind like a cruel loop. *Kind, warm, caring Danny. How could I not have noticed? Isn't a woman supposed to know—feel—this sort of thing? What about my female intuition?*

Although there was no traffic coming from either direction, Maggie automatically clicked on her signal to turn into the driveway of her ranch—and then canceled the signal abruptly. The vet's black GMC was parked near the barn, and she saw Sunday dancing across the back lawn. Danny's head turned at the sound of Maggie's engine, but she was already accelerating, following the road away from her home.

What's the matter with me? she chided herself. *Running away from seeing Danny is stupid and childish and accomplishes nothing. But what could I possibly say to him if Ellie is right? And I know she's right—what I was seeing in Danny's eyes that I thought was a mixture of friendship and sympathy is much more than that. Why didn't I see that?*

Maggie's truck hit a pothole hard enough so that she was lifted off the seat by the impact. A glance at the speedometer told her she was going almost sixty-five on a secondary road that was dangerous at twenty miles per hour slower. She eased the toe of her boot off the accelerator until her speed dropped to forty.

I should've known about Danny's feelings. But how could I? I was a tomboy—my life wrapped up in fast horses and barrel racing. I never even had a real boyfriend before Richie. My friends were gossiping about cute guys and going to dances and parties while I smelled like a hay bale and was spending my time mucking out stalls. I never learned about men.

There was a place—down an overgrown access road to a long defunct cattle operation—that Maggie had found on horseback shortly after she and Rich had bought their ranch. The pulpy, insect-ravaged condition of the leaning fence posts encompassing a large pasture spoke sadly of how long the place had been abandoned. The barbed wire, its spirit rusted away so that the once-sharp points fell to orange flakes and dust when a finger touched them, seemed to have given up when it no longer had any cattle to confine. The remains of a soddy—a simple, cavelike shelter carved into a hill—where the settlers had once lived had seemed a monument to the pioneer spirit to Maggie, and to Rich, when she'd brought him back to see the place.

There was a cemetery too, situated a mile or more from the crude home. Wooden crosses, long since driven to the ground by Montana winds and winters, had been scoured clean of whatever names and dates had been carved into them. One marker, however, was still legible, only because the letters had been chiseled into a flat piece of stone the size of a washboard. It read:

Baby
12-12-1869

Since the day she first saw the single word and the date, they had been etched in Maggie's heart as deeply as they were into the stone. Back then—a mere couple of years ago—Maggie hadn't really experienced grief yet. She'd felt the terrible loss of Baby's parents, but even that sensation had been foreign to her. Now, she believed, she could hold the hands of the man and the woman as a partner to them.

Maggie had a somewhat vague idea how to get to the old homestead from the road, and she knew that attempting to reach the place in her truck would be foolish. The arroyos were deep slashes that were often concealed by the rampant scrub growth, and the rocks and boulders would tear the undercarriage out of her vehicle before she'd gone a hundred yards.

Maggie parked well off the road and set out on foot, climbing a weeded rise. The slope wasn't quite as benign as it had looked through the truck windshield, but the ground was studded with rocks, and the hardy short grass had a firm grip on the soil beneath it, making footing fairly secure. When she stopped to draw a breath about two-thirds of the way to the top, the heat became stifling, saunalike, and the air was as motionless as the inside of a crypt. She wiped the sheet of sweat from her forehead with her palm and shook the moisture from her hand. Then she started upward again, and this time her assault on the rise was an angry one, a fighting mad one, a battle against far more than a hill baking in the sun.

Maggie scrambled upward, dislodging stones and small rocks as her boots fought the magnetism of gravity. She lunged ahead, fell facedown, her palms and knees grinding against the unforgiving surface. That didn't matter—the pain, the chest full of dirt and grit she'd inhaled when she went down—all that counted now was beating the hill, because, at the same time, she was beating the turn her life had taken, the heaviness that had become a part of her, the desolation she experienced daily.

Maggie stumbled over the top and bent forward at the waist, her pulse thudding in her ears, her breath wheezing in her throat as she gasped for air.

There was a flat rock the size of a sofa just over the crest, and even through the shimmer of tears from her sand-abraded eyes, Maggie could see heat radiating from its surface. Next to it, in the selfish bit of shadow the huge rock yielded, was a much smaller flat stone. She collapsed onto it, the jolt of the impact traveling from her seat up her spine like an electrical shock. She let her head fall between her splayed knees and sucked air with all the strength she had left.

After a full five minutes, when she'd blinked and rubbed the grit from her eyes and was breathing freely, Maggie leaned back against the larger rock and pulled a sleeve across her forehead. The knee of her right jean leg was ripped, and the edges of the fabric were wet with blood. Her left palm was bleeding from small cuts, and her shoulders were setting up—stiffening—but not really aching yet.

Dumb. What did that silly explosion prove? Still, a smile crossed her face. *At least I did it, though—it's something I didn't fail at because it was too difficult. That counts for something.*

A pair of jets scribed arcs to the east, the planes themselves silver specks, their contrails exaet, pristine white lines behind them against the unfathomable blue of the Montana sky. Fighter training, her mind told her from the position of the aircraft; one was slightly ahead, with the other to the instructor's right and slightly behind. The lead plane cut away from the follower and began a horizontal climb. The shriek of the engine at full power now reached Maggie but was softened by the distance so that the sound was more like a gush of escaping air than the roar she knew it actually was.

The student plane followed its instructor in the climb. Then, so rapidly that Maggie couldn't see the change in direction, ascent to descent, the fighters blasted back toward the earth. A dull rumble, like thunder from the next county, reached Maggie as the jets breached the sound barrier.

The jets pulled up from their dives again in perfect position with one another and scrambled back in the direction from which they'd come. The sky was marked like the blackboard of an artistic young child, the snowy lines still unchanged, sharp, creating patterns that grabbed and held the eye.

The thought struck Maggie that she'd heard the aircraft from the base daily since Rich died but that this was the first time she'd allowed herself to watch them, to think about them, to let her mind and her eyes follow their paths.

That's something. That's something good. She said a brief prayer for the pilots of the two fighters she could no longer see or hear, and hefted herself to her feet. She wavered dizzily for a moment; her right knee was throbbing now, her body aching. She wiped the blood from her left palm on her jeans and inspected the cuts. They were minor—little more than light abrasions seeping a bit of blood. She shook her head to clear it, not wanting to leave this place, at least not quite yet. Maybe it was the utter solitude or the strange kinship she felt with the settlers who'd lost their child, or perhaps it was the tomblike silence, but this inhospitable and infertile piece of land was where she needed to be, and that was enough reason.

Maggie limped toward the battered soddy, favoring her right leg. What had once been a home was now an overgrown hovel dug into the side of a hill. There was little to see. Supporting timbers had collapsed inside the cavelike excavation, and the interior was thick with scrub growth that had taken root in the dirt floor. She took a shuffling step forward, heard the blood-chilling rasp of a rattlesnake's warning from inside, and scurried backward, the pain of her knee momentarily forgotten. The shade given over the smaller rock where she'd been sitting had grown a bit as the sun moved through the sky, and she returned to her seat and leaned back, closing her eyes.

Ellie's words about Danny Pulver returned to her mind, and with them her own questions about the man.

What do I know about Dr. Daniel Pulver? He's a great vet and I'm in love with his dog. He's from Maine and studied at Cornell Veterinary School. He admitted that Cornell was very difficult and that he had to sweat and grind for the good—although not stellar—grades he got. He's never been married and doesn't seem to be close to the family he left in Maine.

Maggie stretched her right leg out in front of her. There didn't seem to be fresh blood at the tear in her jeans, but the entire limb was throbbing.

Danny was quiet—but he was funny too—at least at times, and with people with whom he felt comfortable. A loner? Maybe. But he'd dated a few locals over the past couple of years. Julie Downs, the reporter at the *News-Express*, had gone to a movie with him a year or so ago, and then, a couple weeks later, to dinner. After that, Julie said he didn't call, and it was clear she wished he had.

A slight breeze moved over the plateau where Maggie sat, and the touch of it against the sweat on her face was delightfully cool.

Could he be in love with me, just as Ellie believes? Is it possible he had those feelings even before Richie died? Maggie shook her head. *He's a Christian. He wouldn't allow himself into a state of covetousness. His faith is too strong.* But suppose he'd gone to Ellie for counseling, and she'd inadvertently—because of her Alzheimer's—shared with Maggie what Danny had told her?

Maggie sighed and stood, using her hands against the big rock to help herself up. Too many questions and not enough answers. She started toward the edge of the rise, realizing that the seat of her jeans was going to take a beating on the way down to her truck, because her right leg was stiff and her knee screamed at her when she put weight on the right side of her body.

Danny's SUV was gone when Maggie parked near her barn, and both Turnip and Dakota were in the small fenced paddock, cropping grass, their coats shining from recent grooming. Maggie limped to the house. A note tacked to the door, written on one of Danny's prescription blanks, fluttered at her. She took it down and read it.

> *Maggie—*
> *I saw you turn away from your driveway earlier. I hope I'm not chasing you away from your own home. Is everything OK?*
> *Danny*

Maggie sighed and went into her house. There were four or five cans of Diet Pepsi and an almost full carton of grapefruit juice in the refrigerator, but Maggie's hand went directly to her big, two-quart Brita pitcher. The water was arctic—so cold that it made her teeth hurt—and she drank thirstily, directly from the spout of the pitcher. The quick chill that embraced her was as delicious as the pure water. As she leaned forward to replace the pitcher in the refrigerator she smelled her body and cringed. She reeked of sweat, dirt, and blood. She hobbled out of the kitchen and up the stairs to the bathroom.

The shower was heavenly, even the stinging part when Maggie let the pressure of the water cleanse the cut on her knee. She reveled in the thick lather of her shampoo and the crisp fragrance of her bath soap as she scrubbed her body. Finally, when the water from the showerhead began to run cooler, coming close to emptying the hot water tank, she shut off the faucets and stepped out into the steam-filled bathroom. She opened the window to clear the air, toweled off, and treated and bandaged her cut, drawing a breath when she dabbed a generous dollop of salve on the wound.

She left the bathroom and went to sit on the couch. The message Dan Pulver had left on her door was on the coffee table in front of her, where she'd tossed it earlier. *Not today, Danny. All I want to do is sit here and relax.*

Maggie closed her eyes for a moment, and the image of the veterinarian appeared in her mind. She heard Danny's voice as he murmured during the exam, soothing the animal, letting him know that everything was OK. Dusty, Maggie recalled, had stood by nervously, shifting her front hooves as she watched this human touch her son. Her liquid eyes flicked to Maggie for assurance but stayed only for the briefest part of a second before returning to the vet and Dancer. Another thought chased the picture from Maggie's mind.

Maybe Ellie is right. It's possible that even before Richie died, Danny had feelings for me. Maybe I knew it on some level all along. The way I'd catch him looking at me and how abruptly—almost guiltily—he'd look away. But . . .

The crunch of tires on the driveway and the sound of an engine brought Maggie to her feet. She walked to the kitchen and peeked through the window, smiling with relief that the vehicle was the Ford truck of Sarah Morrison's groundskeeper, not Danny's GMC. Tessa stepped out, and the truck backed around and rumbled back down the drive, the shovels and tools in its bed clanging against one another. The girl started toward the house, and Maggie opened the door before Tessa reached it.

It was always good to see Tessa. The horse-crazy young girl carried with her a spirit of enthusiasm and plain old happiness and joy that spread to anyone around her.

"Hey, Tessa," Maggie said. "You back to pester poor ol' Turnip again today?"

The girl's smile could have turned a rabid wolverine into a purring kitten. She took a large and shiny apple from the pocket of her jacket. "This is for Turnip," she admitted, "but I really came to talk with you for a minute. Ralph was going to pick up some parts for the mower, so I snagged a ride with him. Are you busy?"

"Busy goofing off is all. Come on in. Want a Pepsi or some coffee?"

"I'd love some coffee, but I've already had my cup for the day. My mom's afraid the caffeine will turn me into a speed freak. A Pepsi'd be great."

Tessa sat at the kitchen table as Maggie fetched a pair of diet Pepsis from the refrigerator.

"You're limping," Tessa said. "Are you OK?"

"I stumbled and scraped a knee is all. No biggie." She set the can of soda in front of the girl. "So, what's up?"

Tessa broke eye contact with her friend, suddenly acting as if her soda can required intense inspection. "Well . . . the thing is, Danny seemed to be upset earlier. He saw you start to turn in the driveway, with your signal on and everything, and he said you saw his truck and drove away." She paused for a moment, still studying her Pepsi container. Her cheeks reddened. "I know I have a major crush on him, but that's not the problem. I'm only a kid, and he's an adult. But what he feels for you isn't a crush."

Maggie waited a moment. "Maybe so, honey," she said softly.

"Danny would just die if he knew I was talking to you like this," Tessa said. "And I don't even know for sure why I'm here, except that both of you are important to me, and I wasn't sure if you realized how he feels."

The kitchen fell silent, and a raucous gathering of crows in a far pasture seemed inordinately loud.

"I'm not unaware of what you've said," Maggie said. "But, honey, Richie hasn't been dead a year yet. I don't know what Danny expects . . ."

"I know you loved your husband a lot, Maggie," Tessa said. She was making eye contact again, and her pain and concern was as apparent as the quiet beauty of her face.

"*Loved* is the wrong word, Tessa," Maggie said, reaching across the table and taking the girl's hand in her own. "It's *love*—present tense—and I don't think that will ever change. Dan Pulver is a wonderful guy, and if things were different . . . but they're not."

They heard a vehicle in the driveway and then a quick tap on its horn. Tessa stood, and Maggie stood with her. "I guess the shop had Ralph's stuff ready for him," Tessa said. "I didn't think he'd be back so quickly. I wanted to explain all this better."

"Thanks for coming to me. We'll talk again, OK? Give Turnip his apple and go on home."

Tessa reached out to Maggie and hugged her tightly.

Words at this point weren't necessary between them. Tessa released Maggie and turned away. At the door she halted and turned back. "He's a cool guy," she said.

Maggie nodded. "I know that."

She watched from the kitchen as Tessa waved to Ralph, said something to him, ran into the barn, and emerged a few moments later. When the truck was gone Maggie went back to her place on the couch in the living room.

A cool guy. As if all that's necessary to fix the hole in my heart is a cool guy. Things are so easy for kids—everything is good or bad, and love conquers all, and everyone ends up with the right person, and no one ever dies testing jet planes.

She closed her eyes and put her head back. The night—Christmas Eve—that Dancer was born drifted into her mind. She remembered the bitter cold of the night, and the panic in Dusty's eyes, and Danny cradling the foal in his arms as if it were a human infant, and Rich's joy at the birth.

Maggie jerked forward, sitting up straight on the couch. In her half dream, Danny's facial features had been as clear and sharp as they were in real life, but Rich's were somehow clouded, indistinct, like the face of a stranger seen from far away.

5

Maggie was as drenched as she'd have been if she were caught outside during a torrential downpour. She was overheated, frustrated, angry, and very tired—and she still had a hundred or more bales of hay to lift, flip, inspect, and restack. She wore a long-sleeved shirt, jeans, and leather gloves, but bits of chaff stuck to her face and in her hair, her nose was so full of hay sediment and dust she could barely breathe through it, and her throat felt as if she'd been swallowing handfuls of broken glass.

The temperature outside the barn was a steady, airless, all-encompassing ninety-seven degrees. Inside the barn it felt like three times that. Indian summer had the entire state of Montana gasping like fish on a riverbank. Maggie hefted a seventy-five-pound bale from the wall of hay in front of her and dropped it at her feet. Even through her almost-plugged nose, the pungent, swamplike stench of mold assaulted her.

Save twenty-five cents a bale, she chided herself. *Buy from a new guy—a young farmer getting his operation started. Great timothy hay—great price.* She grunted as she hauled the bale to the access door in the middle of the second story of the barn and tossed it out into space. It thudded dully when it slammed into the fifty or so bales that'd already been tossed out. One of the strands of baling twine snapped, and a small explosion of grayish dust and bits of stems and plant heads rose into the air.

The dust and the smell told the whole story. The hay had been baled when it was wet, and the process of fermentation had started, rendering the bale not only unfit for feeding horses but also dangerous to their health. Respiratory and intestinal diseases could—and very frequently did—result from feeding what farmers and ranchers called "dusty" hay.

You imbecile—save a crummy quarter a bale . . .

The scene from two days ago replayed in Maggie's mind, the entire conversation etched with acid in her mind.

"I bought from you in good faith," she'd told Troy Hildebrand and his live-in girlfriend, Flower. "Some of the hay is no good. I need you to get it out of my barn immediately."

Troy pulled some stalks from the bale in the bed of Maggie's truck and sniffed it. "Maybe a couple of bales is dusty. That don't mean it's bad hay. Anyway, how do we know you're not runnin' a scam here—tryin' to dump your dusty hay on us, sayin' it was the stuff we delivered?"

Maggie struggled to keep her voice level. "Let's go in your barn. I'll show you some dusty bales."

"All sold out—and we haven't gotten complaints from no one else," Flower said. "Just you."

"Who did you sell to? Someone local? Let's check the hay you supplied to them, then."

Flower's smile was as diseased as the hay she and her lover sold. "Sorry. A distributor for circuses, carnivals, rodeos—stuff like that—bought all we had. Our barn is empty."

"So is the place where you keep your ethics," Maggie had snarled. It had felt very good to say that—and it had accomplished nothing.

The anger that welled in Maggie as she replayed the scene in her mind sent bursts of adrenaline to her weary muscles. In another hour, the moldy hay was gone from her barn, and the good hay was restacked, with plenty of room between the bales to allow the air to circulate more freely. She stiffly eased down the wooden ladder to the main floor, stood there for a moment, and then shook herself like a dog emerging from water. A gritty cloud arose from her, and a paltry few bits of hay dislodged, but the rest clung to her sweaty face, back, chest, and hair as if it were glued there. One more chore—and then the longest, soapiest shower in the world.

A dozen twenty-five pound sacks of agricultural lime rested just inside the barn, where the farm delivery service had dropped them a few days ago. The white powder—used in small amounts to freshen the floors of her stalls—was more economical when purchased in hundred-pound sacks, but those were awkward and difficult for her to lift. The larger sacks were plastic and waterproof, while the smaller ones were paper. Rich had always ordered the bigger ones and stacked them on the shelves with ease.

Maggie opened the door to a series of three shelves where various medications, hoof dressing, and miscellaneous horse supplements, vitamins, and so forth were stored. The top shelf was empty—a perfect place for the bags of lime. She picked up a sack in both hands, lifted it over her head, and guided it to the top shelf. The bottom of the bag swung open, much like a small trap door, with a wet, tearing sound. Twenty-five pounds of pristine, sparkling white lime cascaded down onto her head, shoulders, and body. Coughing, gasping, and flailing her arms wildly, Maggie stumbled out of the barn, her eyes clenched shut. The toe of her boot stubbed against a half bale of hay, and she tumbled forward into the mass of dusty and broken bales she'd tossed down from the second story.

"Maybe this isn't a good time," a male voice called out to her. "I could come back later."

Maggie dragged off her gloves, wet her thumbs in her mouth, and cleared her eyes as well as she could. Through powder, grit, and hay chaff, she focused on the man. He was about six feet tall, trim, with longish sandy-brown hair. His eyes, Maggie saw even through her obscured vision, were blue, but their actual shade was difficult to discern through her tears.

"I'm Ian Lane," he said. "Hey, having a horse farm is really glamorous, isn't it?"

Maggie sat stunned in the hay for a long moment. Then the entire ludicrous situation caught up to her. It was a laugh-or-cry moment, and her sense of humor made the decision for her. Her laughter came in dry, raspy bursts from her parched throat, putting tiny puffs of lime into the air in front of her. The minister laughed too, and the sound was open and warm and sympathetic.

Maggie struggled to her feet, assisted by Reverend Lane's hand taking hers and easing her up. "Reverend," she croaked, "I . . ."

"It's Ian, Ms. Locke. I still look behind me to see who they're talking to when people call me Reverend."

Maggie swallowed hard, trying to clear her mouth and generate enough saliva to say something coherent.

Ian began tapping his loafer on the cement impatiently. "Well, look—let's get to the real reason I'm here. Do you have your purse with you? I'm taking up a collection to install a hot tub and sound system in the home the church provided for me. The suggested donation is—"

"Stop," Maggie begged, the laughter actually painful as it erupted from her parched throat.

Ian smiled. "My extensive training in psychology indicates to me that this may not be the perfect time for a home visit." His grin was broad and innocent and full of fun. "How about tomorrow at about 2:00?"

Maggie, still choking, nodded her head and motioned the reverend to go away—immediately. He too nodded, turned, and began walking to his car. Before he slid into the driver's seat, he waved cheerfully. All Maggie could do was laugh harder and continue motioning him away.

As soon as the reverend's little red Ford left the driveway,

Maggie bolted toward her house. The thought occurred to her that she hadn't laughed with such pure abandon and mindless pleasure in almost a year.

The following day was blessedly cool. A quick and spectacularly vivid thunderstorm had cleansed the air and washed away the grit and dust that the off-season heat had left behind. Maggie's pastures seemed almost impossibly fresh and green, and the white paint of the fences and deep red of the barn looked like it had been applied the night before. The air was pure and wonderful to breathe, and the *clink* of a steel horseshoe against a stone rang out like a bell. The thudding of Dakota and Turnip's hooves on the soil as Danny and Tessa loped across a far pasture echoed back to Maggie in a precise percussive rhythm.

Maggie was in the kitchen brewing fresh coffee when Reverend Ian Lane's Ford Aspire parked next to Danny's GMC. There weren't many compact vehicles in the Coldwater area, and Maggie inspected the car as Ian shut down the engine. It was slightly larger than a VW bug, and the sun glinted on its polished, fire-engine red paint. The car reminded Maggie of an enraged lawn mole for some reason—perhaps because the front end of it appeared to be lower than the rear, like a crouched and menacing varmint. Maggie stifled a laugh. She walked outside to greet Reverend Lane, striding to him and extending her hand when they were close.

"I see you're admiring my car," he said. "I could see you laughing right through the kitchen window."

"I wasn't . . ."

"Sure, it's weird looking," he said, pride obvious in his voice. "But it's almost impossible to get parts for it too. And," he added, "it's under-powered." He took Maggie's hand in his own. His grip was warm and dry and strong without being crushing. There was no agricultural lime in Maggie's eyes, and no hay dust, so she inspected her visitor.

Reverend Lane had a great smile—almost a toothpaste-ad smile—and his eyes were a crisp, intelligent blue. His hair, somewhat shaggy and not at all ministerlike, was a nondescript sandy brown. His face and bare arms were lightly tanned, and he was wearing the same pants he'd had on the day before and a polo shirt. Maggie noticed he was wearing penny loafers without socks. She released his hand and glanced again at the minister's car.

Ian caught the quick flick of her eyes. "I could've had a new Rolls-Royce like Sarah Morrison's," he said. "But I prefer a smaller, more distinctive luxury vehicle."

"You know Sarah and Tessa?" Maggie managed to choke out with her laugh.

"Sure. And I know Danny Pulver too. That's his gas-guzzler there, isn't it?"

"Yep. Danny and Tessa are out trail riding. C'mon—let's go inside and have some coffee."

Ian sat at the kitchen table as Maggie poured coffee. "Where'd all that hay go? From yesterday, I mean?"

Maggie sat across from the minister. "I paid the boy down the road ten dollars to haul it to the dump."

The silence in the sun-bathed kitchen wasn't uncomfortable as they enjoyed their coffee.

Ian spoke again first. "Ellie asked—demanded, actually—that I stop by, Ms. Locke. I talked with her a couple of days ago."

"Please—it's Maggie. How's Ellie doing?"

"She misses everyone. She sounded good. She said you've written to her."

"Yeah. I guess my letters don't say much, but I want her to know I'm thinking of her."

Ian set his cup on the table. He looked into Maggie's eyes, and his spark of humor was gone. "As you know, it'd be inappropriate for me to offer much in terms of counseling, Maggie, at least not on a regular basis. But I want you to know that we have some common ground."

"Oh?"

"I was married for almost six years. My wife and I lived in Chicago, and I had a small church in a tough area. Maria, my wife, ran an abused women's shelter. A guy whose wife and little boy were in the shelter shot and killed her when she wouldn't let him in."

"I'm sorry," Maggie said, her voice a whisper. "Then you know what it's like."

"Yeah." There was a silence. "Maria died almost four years ago, and I still can't really believe it. I find myself thinking it's a nightmare—that I'll wake up. But, of course, I don't." Ian's voice had gone flat, as if the emotion behind the words was more than his voice could handle. "I found one of her grocery lists stuck in a book the other day—Maria made lists for just about everything—and it tore my heart out. It was like the first day all over again, when the police came to my door to tell me what happened."

"Sometimes I wonder how much a person can take without flying apart from the grief," Maggie said quietly.

Ian met Maggie's eyes. "A lot. A great, vast, encompassing whole lot. Life is a gift. The Lord never promised any of us permanent happiness on earth. But—and here's the saving grace—he will give us the strength we need to keep on going if we ask him. I know this is true, because it's what I've done daily since Maria died."

Again the kitchen fell silent, and, to Maggie, the sound of the ticking wall clock seemed louder than it ever had before.

"I'm glad you told me about Maria, Ian—told me about everything."

"I am too, Maggie."

A crow cawed raucously out by the barn and was answered by another from farther away. Ian took a deep breath. When he spoke, his voice was completely different from what it'd been a moment ago, as if he were trying to push away the sadness and longing that had permeated the room. The beginning of the grin on his face wasn't a 100 percent natural, but it was close enough.

He held his cup out to Maggie. "I wonder if I could have some more of this brown, rather bland liquid, Maggie?"

Maggie sat straight in her chair. "Brown liquid? Bland?

I make the best coffee in Montana—and this is a mix of Starbucks and Eight O'Clock Dark Roast. It's . . ."

Ian shook his head sadly. "You poor thing," he murmured. "But I guess we all kid ourselves in one way or another. Look," he said, "I buy a pound of Blue Mountain African coffee each month. It takes most of my salary, but I'm willing to make that sacrifice for good, strong coffee." He paused for a perfectly measured beat. "'Course, I hide the Blue Mountain when company comes. Even my mom has never found it."

Maggie laughed. "You must do that a lot, Ian—use humor to kind of defuse situations. Yesterday I was ready to chew barbed wire and spit nails because of that moldy hay, but once I got to laughing . . . it got better."

"I'll tell you a secret. No, actually, it's two secrets. Maria and I used to sneak into Chicago and go to those do-it-yourself comedy clubs, and I used to perform. My stuff was as amateurish as everyone's, but I always got a few yuks. And I loved doing it. It was kind of unministerial, so we didn't tell much of anyone about it. Then, after Maria was killed, I was seeing a therapist—a grief counselor, actually. He did lots of work with the survivors of cancer and AIDS patients."

The memory of that time, Maggie noticed, brought pain to Ian's eyes. After a moment, he continued. "He told me I should start working humor into my life wherever I could—not sitcom junk or joke book stories, but the silly type of humor that's generated by our own lives or those of the people around us. I thought he was crazy, but I gave it a try. It works. Life is funny stuff, Maggie. It really is."

"Laughter's the best medicine?" Maggie asked, grinning.

"Cheaper than Valium or Paxil."

The drumming of hooves caught their attention. Maggie stood and went to the kitchen window. "Come here, Ian—look at this."

Tessa and Danny were loping along the fence line of the pasture in which Dancer now spent his days after being weaned from Dusty. The colt moved as smoothly as a line of good poetry, his tail flowing behind him like a banner, his hooves seeming not to strike the ground but to flow over it with a balletlike effortlessness. Maggie noticed that Dancer was slightly ahead of the two horses on the other side of the fence, and that Tessa's mount was fighting her for some rein to put himself ahead of the young upstart who was taunting him.

"Is the little guy teasing Tessa's horse?" Ian asked.

"You bet he is—he knows exactly what he's doing. What arrogance!"

Dancer slowed as the fence at the end of his pasture drew near. Turnip, shaking his head and still arguing with Tessa, laid his ears back and showed his teeth as he passed the youngster. Danny and Tessa both laughed at the power play—and so did Maggie and Ian at the kitchen window.

Maggie was suddenly aware of how close she and the minister were standing together—she noticed the scent of his light aftershave and the freshly ironed smell of his shirt. She moved back to the table perhaps a little too abruptly.

Ian waited a moment and then followed Maggie and sat again.

"The young horse is going to be a barrel racer, correct?" he asked.

Maggie poured more coffee. "Right. I think he'll be a great one. There's not much I can do with him until he's two years old in terms of training, but I handle him a lot, pick up his feet, put a blanket on his back every so often."

"I saw some barrel racing on the tube a couple of weeks ago. It's exciting—I liked it. I've never seen the sport live, though."

"It's a lot of fun for the riders, and the horses too. It's a good, clean, fast sport. You ought to—hey!" The words tumbled out before Maggie was completely aware she was saying them. "Tessa's going to run Turnip next Saturday at the October Festival at the fairgrounds. Why don't you come along? It's their first time out together, and Turnip needs the exposure to the arena, the crowd, the noise—all that. Danny's coming too. We'll make a day of it."

Ian's smile was that of a little boy finding his first bicycle under the Christmas tree. "I'd love to. I know as much about horses as I do about brain surgery, and I'm going to have to learn if I want to live here. Sounds great—I'll look forward to it."

"Good," Maggie said. "You can meet us there at about noon on Saturday. I'll be hauling Turnip in my trailer, and Tessa will ride with me. Barring emergency calls, Danny'll be there around noon too." When she looked at the minister, she thought she saw worry on his face. "What? What's the matter?"

Ian squirmed a bit in his chair. "Can Tessa . . . do it OK? She has only one arm, and . . . well . . ."

Maggie smiled. "It's not a strength contest, Ian. Barrel racing is all about skill and balance and speed—and a willing horse that's well trained. The kid is a natural on a horse, regardless of the number of arms she has. It's sweet of you to be concerned for her, but she'll do fine."

Ian's grin returned. "Will she win anything? Turnip looks fast."

"He is fast, and he knows the pattern. But he tends to get silly, and Tessa's going to be nervous. I imagine they'll take down some barrels, but it'll be a good experience for both of them. Next summer she'll do some winning."

The day couldn't have been finer. Fall was obvious in the bite of the chilled air, but the sun was big and benign and the sky was that particularly profound blue that occurs outside of nature only in the perfectly crafted stained glass of cathedrals and churches.

Maggie sat on the fender of her two-horse trailer with her hands around a milkshake-sized Styrofoam container of coffee, the flavor and color of which brought Ian's "brown, rather bland liquid" to mind. She smiled and turned her attention to the arena.

The Coldwater Fairgrounds, built shortly after the end of WWII, was designed specifically for rodeo: four gated chutes for saddle bronc, bareback bronc, and bull-riding contests, a chute on wheels that was pushed into the arena for calf roping, team roping, and steer wrestling, and, of course, a football field–sized expanse of a precise mixture of light sand and good soil that offered excellent footing and traction for horses at speed. Bleacher-type seating surrounded the arena, and tall metal posts with banks of lights on them stood at attention around the huge rectangle for night contests.

All the construction money had gone to the arena, seating, and necessary equipment; the fan parking lot was a vast, rutted, and dusty wasteland that turned to a souplike quagmire when rain came. The contestant parking—another unpaved four acres of poorly leveled ground—was located fifty yards or so from the action end of the arena.

The snack truck had set up in the contestants' parking area early, and although it was only 10:00 a.m., the picnic-like aroma of charring hots drifted about on the sporadic breeze. Perhaps fifty other truck and trailer combinations were parked in a haphazard cluster, and others were banging their way over the potholes and ruts in a steady stream. This was a big day for barrel racers—no other rodeo events were scheduled, and the competition carried National Barrel Racing Association points and prize money.

Some of the trailers were gargantuan four- and six-horse affairs that had bunk space and a small dressing room at the front and air conditioning for both equines and humans. Most were doubles, like Maggie's, but there were more than a few relatively inexpensive singles and several homemades.

Maggie drew in a deep breath. Even over the scents emanating from the snack truck, the rich aroma of shampooed horses, good leather, and the acrid petroleum smell of hoof dressing encompassed the gathering.

Girls and women loped their horses in figure eights in the open acres adjacent to the trailers and trucks, the *thud* of steel shoes against dirt and grass a constant muted drumroll. The riders wore twelve-inch square cardboard numbers safety-pinned to the back of their shirts. Maggie grinned as she spotted the neophytes to the sport; many of the younger girls were almost constantly reaching back to make certain that their numbers were still in place or to adjust them slightly. Those who'd been in more competitions than they could remember were no more conscious of the numbers on their backs than they were of the socks they wore inside their boots.

"Hey, Maggie! Good to see you," a tall redhead called out, swinging down from a flashy steel gray quarter horse. She dropped her reins, told her horse to stand, and rushed forward to Maggie.

"Jackie, great to see you too." The friends grinned for a moment and then stepped back, inspecting one another.

"You look terrific, Maggie," the redhead said. "I've missed you. We've all missed you. Are you riding today?"

"No, I'm not. I hauled Tessa Morrison here. She bought my Turnip."

"I met her. Nice kid. How's Turnip behaving?"

"Real well, but this is their first competition together."

"Big day, then." Jackie smiled. Her horse, standing where he'd been instructed to, raised his muzzle, lips rolled back, nostrils widely dilated, and whinnied long and raucously.

"Twister find a lady friend?" Maggie asked.

Jackie shook her head. "Some bubblehead brought a mare in heat, and Twist is going nuts. If I hadn't watched him be gelded I'd swear he's an ol' range stud. You got any Vicks? I came without mine."

"Sure," Maggie answered, walking to the tack compartment of her trailer. She opened the door, rummaged through miscellaneous gear, and tossed a small blue-green jar to her friend. Jackie caught the jar, unscrewed the cap, and walked to her horse. She used two fingers to dig thick blobs of Vicks from the container. Then she unceremoniously jammed the laden fingers into Twister's nostrils. The horse, startled, reared a bit and then began shaking his head. After a moment he settled down.

"If he can't smell that brazen hussy," Jackie laughed, "he won't pay any attention to her."

"I think he was just looking for a friend—a platonic relationship," Maggie said, straight faced.

"Yeah, like what Anthony wanted with Cleopatra." Jackie rolled her eyes. "I gotta work some kinks out of Romeo here. See you later on, OK?" Jackie recapped the ointment, wiped her fingers on her jeans, and tossed the jar to Maggie. "Don't be a stranger," she said seriously.

Maggie watched her friend pick her way through the trucks and trailers. She put the Vicks back in her tack compartment and began the walk to where contestants were exercising their horses, throwing away her empty coffee cup on her way.

The activity, the horses, the people, the creak of leather, even the patina of anticipatory, pre-event tension, wrapped around Maggie like an old and familiar winter coat on a very cold day. The difference was that Rich wasn't there, grinning, gabbing with friends, sneaking bits of apples to horses.

She took a deep breath, trying to chase away her thoughts.

"Yo, Maggie. Good to see you," a woman on a loud-colored Appaloosa said as she jogged by. Maggie smiled and waved, unsure who the rider was.

I shouldn't be here. It's not right. Even with Tessa and how important this is to her, I shouldn't have come. How can I stay here all the hours I need to? A moment ago, it was all feeling good. Now, I'm as alone as I'd be if the fairgrounds were closed and the day over and everyone else long gone.

Her mind replayed a scene from a couple of days ago, and the memory seemed to increase the weight she felt in her heart.

Danny had brought his check for Dakota's board and a couple of protein supplements for Dusty to Maggie two days ago. They'd sat at the kitchen table.

"We haven't talked much lately," Danny said.

"Well . . . I've been very—"

"Busy." Danny finished the excuse for her. "I know." He sighed. "Sometimes I suppose it's a good thing to keep your feelings a secret, but I'm not good at that. That day I saw your truck start into the driveway and then leave in a big hurry told me something, Maggie. I've thought about it—about you driving off to avoid me—and I'm awfully sorry you had to do that. It's not at all fair to you. Maybe I was being overbearing. I didn't mean to be, but maybe I was." He took a breath and held it for a moment. "I'm not much of an actor, Maggie. I have strong feelings for you. I guess maybe you know that."

Maggie nodded her head slightly without speaking.

Danny cleared his throat. "I can find another place to board Dakota. I'll leave you alone. What I'd like to do is to make your life better, rather than—"

Maggie's hand reached out and covered Danny's without a thought, without her direction. "No, Danny! I don't want you to go away at all."

Their eyes met for a long moment. Danny's voice was heavy with emotion as he spoke. "Then I won't, Maggie. I'll be here for you. And I'll hope and pray that when the time's right, you'll feel about me as I do about you."

Maggie was acutely aware of the sensation of her hand over Danny's—the hardness of it, the rough texture of the flesh, the mounds of his knuckles.

"You have to understand who comes first in my heart, Danny—and that my mind, my life, has turned to . . . to . . . some kind of venomous thing that hates itself so much because it's so alone." Tears came, and Maggie freed her hand and pushed back her chair; the screech of wood against tile was louder than a fire siren in the kitchen and the quiet afternoon.

Danny stood, reached over the table, and used a finger to wipe a tear from Maggie's face. "You're not alone," he whispered. Then he turned and walked to the door. In half a minute, Maggie heard him start the engine of his GMC and roll down the driveway.

I didn't offer anything beyond friendship. Not a thing. But when I was holding his hand . . .

The irritating bleep of a horn directly behind her caused Maggie to turn quickly and return to the present.

"Where should I park?" Ian Lane called to her from his little red car. "I'm afraid that all these trucks will gang up on me if I stop moving."

Maggie's mood shifted as soon as she saw Ian's face. "Put it over by my truck," she said. "Tuck it in close to the side, and don't block the back end of the trailer."

"Sure. I'd be glad to. There's only seven thousand trucks and trailers here. I'm sure I can find yours before the day's over."

Maggie smiled at Ian's frustration. "Is the good reverend using sarcasm? I'm shocked."

"I'll buy you a coffee if you lead me to your truck. How's that?"

"Excellent." Maggie turned around and retraced her path, listening to Ian's compact car bottoming out as it bashed its way behind her. She stopped a few yards from her rig and motioned Ian to it. He snugged his car next to her truck, released his seat belt, and stepped out. He stood still for a moment and then walked toward her, his gait strangely crablike, as if he were stepping on hot coals. Her eyes dropped to his feet.

"Wow. Great boots, Ian."

"They ought to be. I paid a bushel basket of money for them. They felt great at the store in Coldwater, but now they're killing me."

"What kind are they?"

"Justins, which are supposed to be good boots, no?"

"Yeah, but what kind of socks are you wearing?"

"Socks? Just regular athletic socks, I guess. Nobody said anything about socks when I bought the boots."

Maggie bit back laughter. "Have you worn boots before, Ian?"

"Only the galoshes my mom used to buckle for me when I was in grade school." He stood in place, looking like a scolded puppy. "These things hurt, Maggie. I mean it."

"Of course they do—they're brand new. You need to wear slippery socks—silk or whatever—for the first few times. And you need to dust the insides of the boots with baby powder before you haul them on. Good boots will shape themselves to your feet, but with thick socks and no baby powder, all you're going to do is raise blisters and cause yourself grief."

"Swell," Ian grumbled. "No wonder all the cowboys were gunslingers and psychopaths. Their boots drove them to mindless violence."

"It's not rocket science, Ian—all you need to do is break the boots in. Did you bring any other shoes?"

The minister looked suddenly sheepish. "Why would I do that?"

This time, Maggie laughed out loud. "'Cause you knew you couldn't spend a full day in your fancy new cowboy boots. Tomorrow get some baby powder and a pair of slippery socks and wear your boots for a few hours. Do that for a few days, and I guarantee you'll never go back to those yuppie loafers of yours."

"Right now, my yuppie loafers sound like the best thing in the world." Ian turned and went back to his car, dropping into the driver's seat with a grunt-sigh combination that was a pure release from pain. He struggled and teased his boots off and eased his feet into his penny loafers and joined Maggie. "About that coffee I owe you—let's do it."

As they walked to the snack truck and the cluster of people around it, Ian "ahhhed" at each stride. His right hand touched Maggie's left, and she felt her own palm turn toward Ian's to accept it, and then they both pulled back from that contact.

What is this? I want to hold this guy's hand—like a silly teen swept away by infatuation. This is all wrong—completely wrong.

Ian stepped ahead of Maggie and stopped. "What's the matter?"

Maggie's fabricated look of confusion didn't convince either one of them. "What do you mean?"

"Your face just changed—and your eyes got cold or angry or something. I was watching you and . . . I dunno. You went away somewhere else."

"Just a bad moment." Maggie attempted to force a smile, but her face wouldn't cooperate. "Could you go get the coffee? I need a second."

Ian looked at her for a moment longer and then nodded. "Sure. You're OK, though?"

"I'm fine." She took a few steps, stopped, and gazed off toward the riders. *This is absolutely insane. I'm at a horse show with Tessa and some friends. I'm supposed to have a good time—fun—see people I haven't seen, people I like a lot. Where does this stupid guilt come from? I don't even know Ian Lane . . .*

"Hey, Maggie, I brought you some coffee."

Maggie turned to find Danny holding out to her a large Styrofoam cup with steam escaping from its top. His smile was broad and warm, and she was glad to see him.

"Thanks, Dan. I'm gonna be coffee-d to death today. You're early—no office hours?"

"Nope." The vet smiled. "I rescheduled those I had. It was just injections and routine well-animal exams." He tapped the pager attached to his belt. "If this doesn't buzz, I've got the whole day to watch Tessa and horses and eat hot dogs."

"Or watch Tessa and hot dogs and eat horses," Ian said, coming up to them with a large coffee in each hand.

"See what I mean about caffeine overload?" Maggie laughed. "You two know one another, right?" The men set the cups on the ground to shake hands. Danny took an awkward half step toward the minister and nudged one of the cups he'd placed on the ground with the side of his boot.

"That takes care of the extra cup," Ian said, handing one of his drinks to Maggie. "Good to see you, Danny."

"You too, Ian. I didn't realize you were a barrel-racing fan."

"This is my first time, but I've seen some competitions on the tube. It looks exciting. When Maggie invited me I jumped at the chance to see it live."

Maggie wondered if she'd imagined the quick shadow that crossed Danny's eyes, and then decided she hadn't. After just a bit too much hesitation, Danny said, "Great. You'll like it." He looked at Maggie. "How's Tessa holding up? Nervous?"

"Of course," Maggie smiled. "This is a real big deal for her—her first time in competition with Turnip. She's hoping her mom will make it in time to see her run."

"Sarah operating?" Ian asked.

"Yes—but early, according to Tessa. Sarah told her she'd be here."

"That'd be good," Danny said. "C'mon, let's go watch the riders warm up their horses." He turned to Ian. "That's a show in itself."

An artist's palette of colors painted the large open area, with horses of every conceivable color loping, jogging, turning figure eights, or, in short, controlled bursts of speed, galloping. The Western shirts of the women and girls were splashes of reds, greens, blues, and yellows, and every possible shade in between. The hats, invariably carefully molded Stetsons, were bits of a rainbow moving seemingly at random, like brightly painted fireflies caught out in the daylight.

The twelve- to sixteen-year-old competitors tended to stay grouped at one end of the exercise rectangle. There, the hoofbeats were punctuated by quick, nervous, high-pitched squeals of laughter, and the phrase "I love your shirt!" was a sort of mantra.

Tessa was a joyous part of this, sitting atop Turnip comfortably, wheeling him in large circles at a slow lope. She wore her Stetson tugged low in front, shading her eyes from the sun, and her straw-blond hair under her hat flowed over her shoulders.

Maggie waved and caught the girl's glance, and Tessa swung Turnip toward her, Ian, and Danny. Tessa picked her way through the other riders, and when her face was suddenly split by a massive, heartwarming smile, Maggie looked over her shoulder. Sarah Morrison was striding toward them, her smile as broad and as heartfelt as that of her daughter.

Tessa stepped down from her horse, and Danny held Turnip's reins as Tessa embraced her mom. "This is so awesome," the girl gushed. "I love it all. The other girls are great, an' Turnip's working perfectly! I'm so glad you're all here."

"If you were wound any tighter, you wouldn't need Turnip to run those barrels," Ian observed. "You could do it on foot and probably win."

"When do you go into the arena?" Sarah asked.

"In about a half hour the first dozen riders gather at the back gate. Then, when our numbers are called, we ride in and make our runs." Tessa took a breath. "This is so awwwesome!"

"It sure is," Maggie said. "Remember, honey, give the

barrels room. You've been brushing them too close lately. Give Turnip the space he needs to come around. OK?"

Tessa nodded. "I will, Maggie." She kissed Sarah's cheek and took the reins from Danny. Then, quickly, she hugged him.

"Go get 'em, Tess," he said with a laugh. "You burn up that pattern, girl!"

Tessa swung into her saddle and in a moment was threading her way to open ground.

The four adults were quiet for a moment. Finally, Ian said quite seriously, "If the look on that girl's face a few seconds ago is any indication, I'd say that barrel racing is the greatest sport ever invented. She's great, Sarah."

"She's awwwesome," Maggie laughed, stretching the word just as Tessa had moments ago.

Maggie often wondered if there was a particular company that manufactured tinny, static-ridden sound systems and sold them exclusively to rodeo facilities. "The Star Spangled Banner" sounded like a very lethargic—or perhaps intoxicated—Minnie Mouse. The announcer attempted to adjust the speed of the recording, and the final dozen or so words of the song zipped by in perhaps a second.

When they were seated again on the bleachers after the national anthem—Maggie and Sarah, with Danny and Ian at either end of the group—Maggie shifted on the hardwood plank and inadvertently elbowed Sarah. "Wow—you're as tense as a block of steel! This is supposed to be fun, ya know."

Sarah tried a smile that didn't quite work. "This is exactly how I felt when I first held a scalpel over a live patient with my mentor and the head of surgery watching me." She moved her knees and lower body to face Maggie.

"Careful," Maggie warned. "Splinters. It might be embarrassing for you to have to go to a colleague to have wood removed from your derriere. Some of these planks are pretty raw."

This time, Sarah's smile was real. As she started to speak, the music rose and the announcer bleated out the name of the first contestant in the twelve-to-sixteen age group. Sarah swallowed whatever she was about to say and concentrated on the rider with the same degree of intensity she'd have exhibited if she were doing a lifesaving surgical procedure. Danny cheered and whooped with the crowd, and Ian seemed happily transfixed by the action in the arena.

The young riders were good, as Maggie knew they would be. These kids had trained and tuned their horses and themselves to shave seconds—and tenths of seconds—from their runs with the devotion and persistence of a teenaged Tiger Woods endlessly practicing chip shots and putts. What the older barrel racers had that they lacked was experience in real competition and the confidence that comes with that experience—which they were beginning to accumulate today.

Maggie drifted in the familiar and comfortable ambiance of the competition. The excitement of the audience, the cheers and the applause, the sympathetic "oohs" when a rider took down a barrel, the glory of the perfect weather, washed over her like a warm spring breeze after a long and cold winter.

She glanced at Ian sitting next to her on her left. He was leaning forward, hands on his knees, pulling with every part of his being for a chubby redheaded girl on a tall black mare as she turned the final barrel and galloped toward the finish line.

Next to her on her right, Sarah Morrison sat like an obelisk, unmoving except for her eyes, which followed every move of each rider. Danny, to Sarah's right, glanced at Maggie, and their eyes met for a moment. She smiled and so did he.

Danny doesn't much like the seating arrangements. And that tiny bit of—what?—sadness when I mentioned I'd invited Ian to join us. But it wasn't that—wasn't sadness, exactly. Anger? No. Hurt. It was hurt.

Even through the hiss and squeal of the announcer's static, the words "Tessa Morrison riding Turnip" were as clear to Ian, Maggie, Sarah, and Danny as if they'd come through a concert sound system. Sarah started to rise, but Maggie touched her shoulder. "You can't stand up—the people behind you won't be able to see," she said. "Barrel-racing audience rules and regs."

Sarah eased back to her seat without speaking, her face grim.

Tessa and Turnip came out of the chute at a full gallop, Turnip reaching far ahead of himself and dragging long sweeps of ground under him.

"Turnip's head's a little high," Maggie mumbled to herself. "He's not watching that right barrel . . ."

Tessa, leaning far forward in the saddle, cued Turnip for the turn a snippet of a second too early. The buckskin started his turn perfectly but had to interpose a stutter step to avoid crowding the barrel. Even so, his inside shoulder brushed the drum, rocking it.

"Ohhh," Sarah gasped as if she'd been punched.

The barrel rocked a couple of inches for an eternity—and then settled back in place. By then, Tessa and Turnip were long gone, digging toward the first left turn, the horse's head lower now, his eyes—and Tessa's—focused on the red and white drum with the letters NBRA on it as if it were the last thing either of them would ever see. Clods of dirt spewed into the air as Turnip and his rider leaned to the left and blasted around the barrel, as close to it as a coat of paint but not touching it.

Turnip's flight to the final barrel was a thing of beauty that drew applause from much of the crowd. He moved like a greyhound, stretched to his limit, hooves sweeping over the ground, head extended and low, eyes again riveted to the barrel.

It was a good turn—not a perfect one, but a good one—that brought horse and rider around in good position to race home. Tessa's whoop was pure joy as Turnip's awesome power and speed carried them to the finish.

Sarah Morrison's whoop was louder than the applause of the crowd. "Did you see that?" she shrieked.

"We saw it, Sarah," Maggie smiled. "And I'm at least as proud of her as you are."

6

Maggie turned the steering wheel of her truck into the gust that had attempted to muscle the vehicle off the road and onto the shoulder, and looked at the landscape around her. Winters in Montana settled in during late October and early November and didn't relinquish their arctic stranglehold until well into May. The sky took on a cerulean depth that was breathtakingly beautiful and at the same time starkly intimidating, because the depth of the blue was hard, flinty, and offered not an iota of warmth. The hues of this Montana winter were vivid rather than soft and gentle to the eye—the fields of snow, the expanses of dead grass, the naked trees, the diamondlike ice of streams, rivers, and ponds, the endless lines of fence posts sharp-edged under the endless sky.

The intrusive, manic voice of a car dealer offering Thanksgiving specials at the best price ever grated in Maggie's ears, and she snapped off the radio. Sarah and Tessa Morrison were hosting Thanksgiving dinner tomorrow, and Danny and Ian had guaranteed Maggie that if she didn't show up at the appointed time, they'd come to her ranch and physically haul her to the feast. She didn't doubt that they'd do it.

Main Street of Coldwater bustled with pedestrian traffic, with trucks and cars parked in front of each of the stores. Huge cardboard turkeys, cornucopias spilling fruit, and shocks of standing corn with leaves flapping in the wind as if trying to escape decorated the lampposts.

Maggie parked in front of the feed and grain store and used both hands when she opened her truck door. Even so, the pressure against her arms was sudden and strong, almost wrenching the door away from her. As she pushed her way down the sidewalk, tiny pellets of ice stung her face. It was a short distance, but by the time Maggie reached the bakery door, her face was numb.

Kornoelje's Bakery had been a cherished institution in Coldwater for almost seventy years. Owned and operated by a close and loving Christian family, the store had barely made it through the bleakest years of the Great Depression. But it did make it—even though a large percentage of its daily production during those hungry years went over the counter to those who had no way to pay or was taken to the church for the soup kitchen there.

The warmth and the delightfully sweet scent in the bakery embraced Maggie like the hug of a grandmother for a favored grandchild. The individual aromas of spice, chocolate, fresh bread, sugar cookies, and pumpkin and apple pies, and the yeasty sharpness of fresh dough being shaped on the huge wooden table in front of the ovens created an ambiance that was perhaps too heavenly to exist in an imperfect world.

Maggie waited in line behind the glass-fronted wooden display case, nodding to people she knew, smiling at the kids begging their parents for cookies. The youngsters behind the counter—family members—hustled about filling bags, wrapping pies and cakes, counting out various treats, giggling, and colliding with one another frequently.

Nevertheless, customers were served quickly and efficiently—and joyfully. Maggie wondered if any facial expression other than a smile could prevail in the bakery, and decided that it couldn't.

Lonnie, a senior in high school, greeted Maggie over the counter. "It's great to see you, Maggie. Made up your mind yet?"

"You too, Lonnie," Maggie said. "How about a dozen cannoli and a loaf of your unsliced Jewish rye." The cannoli were part of Maggie's contribution to the Thanksgiving meal. The loaf of bread was for Maggie herself—and she'd tell anyone who'd listen that it was the very best rye bread in the world, including that from the famous Jewish delis in New York City.

Lonnie handed over the white box containing the cannoli, the loaf of bread in brown butcher paper, and a single oversized chocolate chip cookie. "I remembered these are your favorite, Maggie. Happy Thanksgiving."

It was a simple and kind gesture, Maggie realized, and she was thankful for it. But the gesture exemplified the people and the life in Coldwater, Montana. She spoke from behind a sudden lump in her throat when she said, "Thanks, Lonnie—and happy Thanksgiving to you and the family."

The wind snarled at Maggie as she left the bakery and eased the door closed. She clutched her purchases against her chest like a girl with schoolbooks, feeling the warmth of the bread emanating through the brown paper. Her gift cookie rested on top of the cannoli box. She began down the sidewalk toward her truck and then stopped suddenly, halted by an image that was more real than the town around her. She turned her back to the bakery picture window and stood, transfixed.

We were right here a year ago today. We bought an apple pie and a pumpkin pie, a loaf of rye, and a dozen chocolate chip cookies. Richie ate five on the way home, and I ate three.

We had the Cheap Thrills *cassette in the tape deck in the truck, had it cranked up to the top, and we were singing the blues with Janis Joplin—really getting into the songs, making our voices whiskey-harsh, stretching words and phrases, dragging the sadness, the despair, out of the lyrics. I was patting my knees as if they were drums, and Richie had his right arm across my back and was tapping along with those wonderful guitar runs, and we were as unself-conscious as a pair of children laughing together.*

And as soon as the last notes of "Me an' Bobby McGee" ended, Richie took his arm from behind me and shut off the tape. Then he touched my face very gently.

"We can't be blues singers, Maggie," he said, quite seriously.

"Oh?"

"Real blues people live their music, like Janis and Muddy Waters and Leadbelly did. I can't do blues because I'm the happiest, most fulfilled man in the world, with a wife who's a gift from God. There's no room for blues in my life. None at all—there's too much happiness. And it'll be like this for—"

"Maggie? Are you OK? You must be an icicle by now—you've been standing here for ten minutes. Do you want to come on inside and have some coffee in the back room with me?"

Maggie blinked fast several times, disoriented. She looked down at her packages. The chocolate chip cookie had been stolen by the wind, flipped away to the grime and salt on the sidewalk.

"I'm OK, Lonnie," Maggie said. "I've got to get back to the farm. You go on inside before you freeze. I'm fine—really. I was just remembering . . ."

"Can you drive? Why not sit down for a minute and drink some coffee?"

"I really can't. I've got horses to feed and chores to do. Don't worry, I'm OK; I was just spacing out for a minute. Thanks for coming out—and you'd better go on in before your brothers and sisters give away the store."

Lonnie finally smiled. "Yeah. You take care, Maggie."

Maggie smiled, waved, and fought the wind to her truck. She started the engine and let it idle for a minute before putting on the heater and driving off. *A few months ago what I just relived would have torn my heart out. It hurt today, but I can treasure that moment—at least a bit. No—a lot.*

It was unusual for the horses to be clustered at the back of the barn at midday. Dakota stood tail into the wind; Dancer stood next to him, using the older horse for a windbreak. Turnip danced in place, wide-eyed, and whinnied as Maggie hustled from her truck to the barn. Happy pawed at the dirt in front of the door as if she were attempting to dig her way to safety. Dusty, also wide-eyed, wheeled back, ears flat to her head, teeth snapping, as Turnip tried to shove her away from the closed door. Dancer tucked himself closer to Dakota.

The barn was as cold as a meat locker, and its structure creaked as the wind assaulted it. Maggie knew that a certain amount of flex was engineered into any building, from skyscrapers to garages. Still, the painful-sounding groans of wood grinding wood and the shrill shrieks of her barn were disconcerting, like the cries of an injured animal. The thudding noise at the back door told her the horses were jostling one another for position, anticipating her swinging the door open.

Maggie opened the gates to each of the stalls as she hurried to the back door. She'd mucked the stalls before leaving for town that morning, and each had fresh water, hay, and grain. Horses knew their own stalls from those of their peers; stalls were their safe havens where there was always safety, food, and security. On this day, as Maggie slid open the door on its track and Turnip, Dusty, Dancer, Happy, and Dakota muscled their ways into the barn, all five horses had sudden memory lapses and stood in a nipping, tail-wringing cluster, like a gaggle of nervous chickens. Maggie snatched a lead rope from a hook on the wall and draped it over Dancer's neck, pulling him into his stall. Dakota hurried into Turnip's stall, while Turnip pushed into Dusty's. Dusty, looking confused and frightened, stood gawking at Maggie until she led the mare into Turnip's stall. Happy ended up in her own home and stood tight to the far wall, trembling. The safe haven of their individual stalls no longer mattered to the spooked and nervous animals—any stall was fine, as long as it was inside the barn. Maggie walked from horse to horse, touching each one, speaking softly, offering treats from the basket of apples she kept filled in the barn. Slowly, the animals calmed, and soon each was crunching away at the fresh feed in the grain buckets or on the flakes of hay each stall contained.

Maggie watched her horses eat for ten or fifteen minutes, constantly aware of the power of the wind howling outside. She left the lights on, and before she left the barn she took a long coil of cable-reinforced rope from a cabinet. Outside the barn, less than a foot from the door, a series of stout brass eyes were bolted to the barn wall, the first a foot above ground level, the second two feet, the third three, and the fourth five feet from the ground. She tied a very careful double knot to the third eye and started toward the house, staggering in the wind and uncoiling the rope as she trudged ahead. There had been little snow so far that winter, but Maggie knew that when it came, it would come hard and fast. When lashed by the gale-force winds, snow could obliterate visibility and confuse a rancher who set out to the barn to feed stock.

Rich had read a story about a young Montana rancher who'd been found frozen to death within twenty feet of his home. That same day, Rich had driven to the Coldwater hardware store and purchased the reinforced rope and the brass eyes and fittings. He'd installed them that evening. Maggie kept another coil of the rope in the mudroom so that it could be attached at the house.

Maggie tied another double knot and secured the rope to the house. The strange moaning sound the wind produced as it stretched the rope made her shiver in a way that had nothing to do with the cold. After tying the rope she went to her truck to retrieve her treats and her bread and sighed with genuine relief when she entered her kitchen. When she dropped the bread on the counter it clunked as if she'd dropped a brick instead of a loaf of rye—it was frozen solid. She turned on the kitchen radio before taking off her scarf and coat, catching an already started newscast.

"... up to sixty miles per hour, which is one heck of a lot of wind, even for around here," the announcer said. "But the good news is that the storm is going to miss the Coldwater area, at least for now. The travel advisory is still in effect—all unnecessary travel should be avoided till the advisory is cleared. The National Weather Bureau tells us there's a real good chance the whole mess will veer off and give ol' North Dakota some grief. The wind should taper way down after midnight, and so far, Thanksgiving in our part of the Big Sky State is lookin' just delicious!" He paused for a brief moment, during which his voice took on a cloying semblance of a man-to-man tone. "Ya know gents, lots of us in our thirties, forties, and fifties are losing more hair than we want to—and more than we have to! That's right—you heard me. You don't have to lose your hair, and you can grow back what you've already lost. How? Just listen up an' let me tell you about a new product developed in the scientific laboratories of—"

Maggie snapped off the radio, mumbling, "Idiot," under her breath.

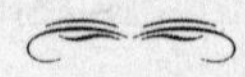

That night something tugged Maggie from a sound sleep. She listened carefully, her eyes finding the clock on her bedside table. The square, liquid green digits read 4:12.

Everything was quiet in the house—just as it should be. Then it struck her: she wasn't reacting to a sound but to the lack of sound. The wind had stopped.

Maggie leaned from her bed and pushed the window curtain aside. Her land, her fences, all of the outdoors slept peacefully under the soft light of a cloudless sky from which a pure white half-moon stood guard. She turned away from the window, adjusted her pillow, snuggled up under her covers, and returned to sleep.

The horses that morning were oddly subdued. Turnip, the most vocal of the four, rarely failed to greet Maggie with a whinny and a snort through his nostrils. Dusty invariably rushed to the front of her stall, awaiting her morning scratch and a few words from Maggie. Dakota, a chowhound who ordinarily followed Maggie's every move with his eyes and grumbled at her as she scooped grain and broke flakes of hay from bales, stood back from his stall gate, showing no interest in his coming meal. Dancer, obviously nervous, his ears moving about too rapidly, his eyes darting just as quickly, was in the far corner of his stall, crouched slightly. As Maggie watched, a slight tremble showed in the colt's neck and shoulders.

Cringing—my most curious and intelligent horse is cringing like a mouse cornered by a cat.

She went into the stall and approached Dancer slowly, her hand extended. When she was in front of him, he moved forward a step and shoved his muzzle into her unzipped coat. She felt him tremble once again. Her practiced hands moved over Dancer, feeling the tension in his muscles, the slightly elevated rate of his heartbeat, the unusual jerkiness of his motions. She murmured to the colt for several minutes, stroking him, still examining him for any indication of sickness. When she backed away from Dancer he moved again to the far corner of his stall.

After Maggie had filled the grain bins and tossed fresh hay into the stalls, Dakota was the first to begin eating. His grunting and crunching apparently activated the appetites of the others, and soon all five were busy with their hay and grain. Maggie examined each of the horses as carefully as she had Dancer. She found no sign of illness or pain. Perplexed and worried, she ran from the barn to her house.

She dialed Danny Pulver's number, and when he answered she breathed a prayer of thanks. It took only moments for her to describe the symptoms of the animals.

"You're the third caller this morning about the same thing, Maggie," the vet said. "What's going on is that the horses are simply reacting to the change in the weather. That wind yesterday afternoon and last night had every animal around here as skittish as a long-tailed cat in a room full of rocking chairs."

"But the wind stopped hours ago. Why are they still reacting to it?"

"Because the barometric pressure has been all over the place and they feel the changes—and it scares them. Look, you know how some dogs get hinky long before thunderstorms, hiding under beds, panting, all that? The thing with the horses amounts to the same thing. Their instincts tell them something is wrong, but they don't quite know what it is. I'll bet Dusty and Dancer and the whole bunch of them came to the barn early yesterday, right?"

"Yeah—yeah they did. It was about midday."

"See? Every horse for miles around was seeking out shelter yesterday. Instinct again, Maggie. I'd suggest you leave them in the barn today and tonight and then turn them out tomorrow morning, just like always. You don't have a thing to worry about. There's nothing wrong with the horses."

Maggie's voice was a bit tentative. "You're . . . you're sure?"

Danny chuckled. "As sure as I am that I'll be real pleased to see you in a few hours at the Morrison's place. OK?"

"OK, Danny. And thanks."

If Danny had been standing there, Maggie would have hugged him. She decided to allow herself the luxury of another cup of coffee, and as she stood at the sink rinsing the pot, she glanced out the window at the rope she'd strung between the barn and the house the night before. She grinned; it looked like a foolishly low clothesline. As Maggie watched, a few fat snowflakes drifted downward lazily, as if they were ambling to the ground rather than actually falling. Soon, her coffee was perking.

Sarah had said noon, and folks in and around Coldwater didn't play the "fashionably late" game. Maggie, after another visit to the horses, was on the road by twenty to twelve, her white box of cannoli in the passenger seat next to her. All of the horses had accepted the apples she'd given them, but they—particularly Dusty—had been needy, wanting more words and more stroking. Maggie topped off their water, tossed extra flakes of hay into their stalls, and left the barn, feeling much like an uncaring and negligent mother.

She turned on the radio as soon as she'd left her driveway. The tiny gospel station from Coldwater was a raucous buzz of static, and she punched in CLTR, the most powerful station.

". . . hate to say this, but it's more'n a little possible, folks. We here at CLTR know lots of our listeners have places to go for the holiday—but I'm askin' you personally—don't do it. The people at the National Weather Bureau have upped their advisory to a warning. It looks like the reprieve from yestiddy has pulled kind of an ugly U-turn and is heading right back at us. 'Member '89 when our cattle . . ." There were no more words.

Maggie turned up the volume, but the screeching, power-saw attack of static hit her like a slap, and she jabbed the off button. She turned into Sarah Morrison's long, serpentine driveway and followed the gentle curves to the house. Ian's silly compact was parked in front, Danny's GMC right behind it. Sarah's Rolls-Royce watched over the lesser vehicles from its garage, its shiplike prow pointing outward down the driveway.

Maggie nudged her truck behind Danny's truck and turned off the engine. *This might be very good. And I need these people.*

She sat for a moment and then tugged upward on the door release. She watched, stunned, as the door slammed forward and crashed against the fender, and then hung twisted from its lower hinge.

The howl of the wind was horrendous—a tidal wave of sound that she felt as much as heard—and assaulted Maggie with battering-ram strength. Her entire body began trembling immediately, and her teeth clattered together with enough force to send shards of pain radiating through her face. It had been cold earlier, but the temperature in the cab of Maggie's truck was now something completely different, unworldly, a frigidity that could snuff life as easily as water kills the flame of a candle.

Maggie could see nothing. There was no definition to

anything around her or beyond her. Everything, including the interior of her truck, was a rapidly swirling, featureless mass of white. Her sense of sight—the most used and relied-upon physical sense humans possess—had, in the tiniest part of a second, abandoned her. She huddled behind the steering wheel of her truck, hands pressed ineffectually against her ears. Her shoulder harness dug into her body as she cringed forward against the restraint, disoriented, in full panic. She may have screamed, but there was no way her voice could register over the wrath of the storm.

It hit like a hunger-crazed, marauding grizzly in a pioneer cabin. The storm struck in all directions at once, tore down trees that had stood through a half century or more of Montana winters, ripped TV antennas from roofs, and scattered satellite dishes from their allegedly impervious foundations. Outbuildings—sheds, freestanding garages, cattle shelters—whirled off, some intact as they stood, others in pieces, never to be seen again.

The sole telephone booth on Main Street leaned with the wind, hesitated, and then wrenched away from the bolts that held it to the cement and flipped over itself three times before it careened off the top of a parked FedEx truck and ultimately shattered against the stone façade of the Coldwater Bank & Trust.

Cattle instinctively huddled tightly together. Three- and four-hundred-pound calves were blown from their feet by the strongest gusts as they hustled to the clusters of the heavier animals, white-eyed and bawling with fear.

The six feet by four feet metal-edged sign in front of Coldwater Church listing times of services was ripped away from the ground and flung two hundred yards into town, where it sheared the top several feet off a mercury vapor light stanchion in the parking lot of Coldwater Power and Gas.

Rough, clutching hands poked and grabbed at Maggie, and instinctively, she tried to fight them off. A sharp slap registered on her cheek and in her mind, and then Danny Pulver's face was inches away from hers—and Ian Lane was fumbling at the release of her seat belt. Danny hollered into her ear, "The house—we've gotta get to the house. Now! Come on, Maggie!"

The seat belt whirled into its retractor, and the two men tugged Maggie from the driver's seat into the full force of the wind. She stood between them, her arms linked with theirs, and they all leaned clumsily forward into the power of the storm.

The snow was a type that Maggie had never experienced. The flakes were small and crystalline and stung exposed flesh like wind-driven sand. There was a frightening density to the snow; it made them gasp for breath as if the very oxygen that sustained life had been dashed away by the snow and wind. During the strongest blasts the visibility was virtually inches and the churning snow seemed to dissolve any concept of direction. The floodlight over the back door of the Morrison home offered only the faintest corona of light, and they trudged toward it like ships struggling through gigantic swells to a safe port.

At the moment the light went out, Maggie's foot tangled with that of Ian and he fell, dragging her and Danny down with him, their arms welded together with the strength of panic and desperation.

The storm howled at their ludicrous attempts to get to their feet, taunting them with its strength. Maggie realized that their links to each other were their links to life itself. Their weight was what saved them from being flung about like chickens in a tornado, but they had another enemy now: directions were totally obscured by the whiteout. Maggie took a step along with Ian and then felt a wrenching at her other arm when Danny tried to set off on an opposite course.

One of the men—she thought it was Ian, but she couldn't see his face, which was a foot away from her—pulled the other two together, heads close.

"This way—I'm sure it is! When we went down I kept facing the way we were going."

"So did I—and you're going away from the house!"

Maggie's face was already numb from the subzero temperature and the wind. She no longer felt the scourging snow, and her feet in her Western boots were clumsy blocks of frozen wood.

"Look—wait—we gotta . . ."

"It's this way. I'm sure of it, Dan. We . . ."

Danny's voice—she could tell it was his because his face was touching her own—was strident now, and the words rasped from his throat at the top volume he could project. ". . . if I have to knock both of you down and drag you there, Ian! I mean it—I'll . . ."

Ian's voice, more of a screech than a shout, came from a few inches from Maggie's face, but she could barely see him. "You're wrong!"

The clanging of a bell was the most welcome sound Maggie had ever heard. The two notes, unmelodious but plainly audible, pealed rapidly. "Sarah's bell!" Ian hollered. "Thank God."

The trio lumbered toward the sound; Ian tripped over something and went to one knee, but the others remained upright and hauled him back to his feet. Clutching one another with aching arms, they passed the corner of the house, and blocked by the building, they felt the wind diminish slightly. Ten feet ahead they could barely see a figure in red cranking the lever on the antique bell. They stumbled to the figure, still not daring to release one another.

Tessa had her back to Maggie and the men. When they touched her she shrieked and spun to them, forcing words through her bloodless lips. "Here! Here—this way!"

The old-fashioned wooden door that opened like the flap of a box from its almost ground-level position had whirled off in the clutches of the storm. Tessa led her friends down the stone stairs.

The normal, year-round temperature in the basement was about fifty degrees. The missing door allowed the storm to immediately drop the temperature to below twenty. The cellar was as dark as a crypt, with the wind whistling through like an express train—and to Maggie it was the most beautiful and welcoming place in the world. A cone of light appeared, and Sarah, holding a six-cell flashlight, rushed to them across the hard-packed dirt floor. She spoke quickly but calmly, in the tone of voice Maggie imagined she'd use during a crisis in the operating room.

"There's a good fire in the fireplace and I've collected blankets. Let's hurry now—we don't want to give frostbite or hypothermia a chance. Hurry—you need heat."

Maggie's face, mere moments ago without sensation, now felt aflame, and her hands and arms trembled almost spastically. "Leave your coats here," Sarah said as they entered the kitchen, "and then get to the fire. Don't sit too close to it—your skin won't be perceiving its heat for a time. Take off anything that's wet and get your boots and socks off as soon as you can. Wiggle your toes. Hurry, now."

The gentle flames of flickering candles spread light throughout the Morrison home. They seemed to be everywhere—standing in dinner plates, in formal silver candleholders, and on saucers. "The realtor told us about the storms and how the electricity goes out, so we bought a case of candles at the hardware store the day we moved in," Sarah said in answer to the unasked question.

The fireplace of original stone in the living room was a thing of beauty, spreading its warmth throughout the room. Sarah had tugged a couch close to the flagstone apron, and a kettle of water boiled over the flames, suspended from one of several hand-forged hooks that had been installed when the home was built well over a hundred and twenty years ago.

Maggie, Tessa, and Danny collapsed onto the couch, pulling quilts and blankets around themselves, Sarah tucking in loose edges. Ian remained standing, his face blotchy red as his circulation returned.

Sarah's medical tone was gone and her words were now those of a mother and a friend. "I'm so glad that bell was so important to me when I first saw it." She smiled. "Even Ellie said I was crazy when I told her how much it was going to cost to have it sandblasted and cleaned and how much the carpenter wanted to build the frame and rehang it." She laughed. "Tessa and I don't have any cowhands or workers in the field, and there are no raiding Indians. But I fell in love with the bell, and now I'm so happy that I did."

"Kind of providential, no?" Ian said.

No one disagreed with him.

It was a feast of sorts, even if Sarah's twenty-two-pound turkey remained in the electric oven, barely half cooked. Canned soup heated just fine over the fire in the fireplace, and crackers and peanut butter were perfect appetizers before the main course of tuna sandwiches on slightly stale white bread. Cold cuts, potato chips, Diet Pepsi, a large bag of salted-in-the-shell peanuts, a tin of anchovies, and most of a bag of Oreo cookies were strange fare for Thanksgiving dinner, but the candlelit buffet had a certain charm all its own. And the black olives, fresh carrots, broccoli, and celery were, everyone agreed, excellent.

Tessa's portable radio brought news from the outside into the Morrison home, but the news was grim. Through the hissing of static and over the relentless pounding of the storm and the rattling of windows, the announcer's voice faded in and out.

". . . since the storm of February 1916. Don't bother with your cell phones, folks. The tower was knocked . . . roads impassable . . . no vehicular traffic of any kind . . . winds of seventy-five miles per . . . minus twenty-six degrees . . . expected for seventy hours . . . snowfall up to . . . National Weather Bureau . . . and stay where you are . . . we repeat . . ."

Danny, easing a log into the fireplace, glanced at the quickly diminishing pile of wood. Tessa followed his eyes. "We just had two cords delivered this week. We're in good shape."

Danny straightened from the fireplace and brushed his hands together over the flames. "Where's it stacked?"

"On pallets under a tarp just outside the main basement door. It's easy to get to—you hardly have to go outside."

"Good," Danny said. "The tarp's probably long gone, but if the wood is stacked decently, it'll be there."

"Our diet won't be fancy," Sarah said, "but we have a ton of soups and other canned goods in the pantry, and there's rice and noodles and spaghetti and all sorts of things. We have more pots and pans than Kmart, and we'll cook in the fireplace." She paused for a moment. "One other thing—we can flush the toilet by dumping pails of melted snow into it. It's not genteel, but it'll be sanitary."

"Will that work?" Tessa asked.

"Sure," Danny answered. "It's a kind of a gravity thing, actually. You need electricity to pump water to the toilet tank, but once the water is there and the toilet is flushed, it should work. I have the same system at my place." He shook his head. "This thing came on without warning. Lots of cattle are going to die where they stand before it's over."

Tessa looked at Maggie with fear in her eyes. "The horses," she said. "What about the horses?"

"Yeah," Danny added. "I've got an awfully good dog in a mudroom with only a pan of water and his morning meal."

Maggie forced a half smile onto her face. "The horses will be fine, Tessa," she said, avoiding looking at Danny. He knew as well as she did what hungry, thirsty, storm-panicked horses could do to themselves in a closed barn.

A moment of uncomfortable silence hung over the room until Ian broke in. "Danny, how about if we haul some wood in? We might as well get that taken care of and make sure we have enough up here to get us through the night."

Danny stood. "Good point. Let's do it."

"Are your things dry yet?" Sarah asked. "You don't want to be working in damp clothes."

"Real men—like veterinarians—don't notice the elements. We strong like bool," Danny added in a harsh, heavily accented voice.

"Ministers notice, though," Ian said. "I could use a sweater under my coat if anyone has a spare one."

"One thing we have is a ton of sweaters," Tessa said. "As long as you're not too particular about the fit, we can fix you up."

"It's not the fit I'm concerned with," Ian said seriously, "but the color, and how it coordinates with what else I'm wearing."

Maggie played along. "Good point," she said dryly. "How's this—the ladies will close their eyes, and Danny doesn't much care, so you should be OK."

A few minutes later the clunk and clatter of logs hitting the dirt floor of the old basement added a new sound to the racket of the storm. Danny and Ian worked hard and fast, not bothering to stack the lengths of wood in the frigid, doorless basement, since after being brought inside, the wood needed to be hauled up the stairs to the fireplace. If there was conversation between them it didn't register upstairs. Maggie and Sarah sat on the couch, each lost in her own thoughts. A loud snap as a knot burst in the flames seemed to awaken both women from their introspection.

Tessa dropped an aluminum bowl onto the ceramic tile floor of the kitchen, and the sound rang through the house like a bell, as did the girl's exasperated "Rats!"

Sarah moved a bit closer to Maggie. "You heard that 'real men' bit, didn't you?"

"Just a joke," Maggie answered in a low voice, barely louder than a whisper.

"Semi, Maggie—a semi-joke, at best."

A long moment passed. "Yeah," Maggie said. "I guess you're right."

"You know how those two feel about you, don't you?" Sarah found Maggie's eyes with her own. "Ian is less obvious than Danny is, of course. Ian runs deep, Maggie, and he's protective of his heart, but the feelings are there. You can take my word on it—I don't miss things like that. My point is that there are two very good and very different men interested in you."

"I suppose so. It's just that I don't know what to do about it."

"Not a terrible position for a young woman to be in," Sarah said. "All in all, I mean—and after some time passes."

Maggie sighed but didn't speak.

"Gonna be a long storm, no matter how long the weather lasts," Sarah said.

7

The storm never quite became background noise.

The house shuddered and creaked and rattled and moaned under its virulent pummeling, and the occasional pockets of quick silence as the wind careened in from a different direction were somehow louder and more frightening than the storm's onslaught. During those moments the snow—already accumulated to almost three feet—presented a bizarre panorama of gentle-edged sculpture, with sweeping, four- and six-foot waves lapping at the sides of the old house, and a barren spot of brown, dead grass the size of the Thanksgiving table of a large family surrounded by sloping, solid walls of snow. After the moments of respite, the wind destroyed its handiwork like a cranky and spiteful child but began rebuilding again immediately, shaping new drifts and images.

"I saw a storm in the Sahara that was like this, except with sand," Sarah said, stepping back from a window. "It made me feel very small and insignificant, but I don't think it scared me like this does."

"This house has seen stuff like this before, Sarah," Danny said. "We couldn't be in a better place—we have shelter, food, and heat. We'll wait it out."

"I don't think we have a choice in the matter," Maggie said. "But Danny's right—we couldn't be in a better place." After a moment, she added, "Or with better people. Suppose we weren't all such good friends? As big as this house is, things would get awful tight if we didn't get along so well."

Ian waited a moment. Then he snarled, "Will you please stop your nagging, Maggie? You're driving us all nuts!"

Danny, at first startled by Ian's outburst, joined in. "Tessa, your giggling grates on me like fingernails on a blackboard. Go to your room, ya little twerp!"

"At least my clothes don't smell like a wet dog," Tessa said. "And how about sharing that box of Cheez-Its you have hidden in the dining room?"

Sarah and Maggie's eyes met, and both of the women smiled. Sarah sighed. "All three of them are fourteen, Maggie."

"I noticed that," Maggie said. "And it's a young fourteen too."

For a while, the snapping of the fire and the voice of the storm were the only sounds in the candlelit room. Tessa broke the silence.

"I think it's fair to say that I'm the best Monopoly player in the world, and I know right where my game is."

"You're awfully young and filled with childish notions, Tessa," Ian said. "It's really part of my ministerial obligation to help you see the truth, even if it hurts your pride."

"Wait a minute here, folks," Danny said. "Do you think I've amassed my vast fortune, my real estate empire, my international reputation, through luck?" He sighed dramatically. "Monopoly is too easy for me. But I'll play—at least to teach you all a lesson about finances."

Maggie cleared her throat. "I'd like to play," she said in a falsely plaintive voice, "but my checking account is down to six dollars. Does that disqualify me?"

"I want to be the banker," Sarah demanded.

It was an interesting, if somewhat freestyle, game. About halfway through, Maggie paid Danny five hundred dollars to take her turn to fetch wood from the basement for the fireplace. Grumbling, Danny got the wood. Twenty minutes later he agreed to lend Maggie a thousand dollars—but she was required to go to the pantry immediately and scrounge for snacks for the players.

Sarah played conservatively and accumulated an immense wad of cash—which she was forced to hand over to Tessa when she landed on her daughter's Park Place with four houses on it. On the next roll, Ian landed on the same square. When he refused to pay Tessa's usurious lending rates, Tessa forced him into bankruptcy. When Maggie was caught attempting to surreptitiously slide Ian a few hundred dollars, she was fined two thousand dollars and forced to miss two consecutive turns by Sarah, the flint-hearted banker. During that time, Maggie wasn't allowed to collect if others landed on her properties.

Danny was forced out of the game by two disastrous landings on Tessa's holdings. Maggie soon followed him. Sarah was cash-rich but held few property cards, and those she did own were piddling things—a railroad, Baltic Avenue, and a couple of others. Tessa whittled her mother into the poorhouse in a matter of a half dozen rolls.

"See?" The girl grinned. "I told you."

The hilarity of the game dwindled away. The weather had worsened; the wind was a painful shriek and the house shuddered under its assault. Sarah wandered off to the kitchen, and Maggie followed her. The light from the two candles cast a deceivingly warm glow to the room, which was cold, just like every other room of the house but the living room.

"We should probably put these candles out," Sarah said. "We don't know how long we're going to be without light. We have most of a case of them . . . but still . . ."

"Yeah," Maggie said. "Maybe so. Do you have enough matches?"

Maggie could see Sarah's smile from across the room. "I completely forgot about matches, but Tessa bought a half dozen boxes of those strike-anywhere kind. So, yes, I'm sure we have enough."

"Good." Maggie looked toward the living room, heard voices, and turned back to Sarah. "I'm scared. I really am. My stomach is trembly, and every time a gust hits I jump."

"We're all a bit scared, I think—even the guys. But we'll get out of this OK. I know we will. Danny's like a mountain man—he knows what to do in emergencies, and Ian's one of the brightest men I've ever met. Before this is over, I think his sense of humor is going to be as important as firewood.

And you, Maggie—you're tougher than you think you are. You're a gutsy lady."

"I wish."

"No, I mean it. You've been through a whole lot of trouble, and you've picked yourself up after you were knocked down. That takes strength."

Maggie leaned against a counter and picked a pretzel out of a bowl. As she nibbled at it, Sarah moved a step closer to her. "I think your strength is a large part of what Danny and Ian see in you."

"That's another problem," Maggie said. "I can't control their feelings, but at times I want to scream at them that it's too soon for me to become involved in a relationship again. And, even if I wanted to, which one of them would I choose? They're both great guys, and if something does happen, one of them's going to get hurt."

"People get over hurt," Sarah said softly.

"That's what I've been told." Maggie sighed. "Let's go out by the fire. It's like an igloo in here."

"In a second. Just let me say one more thing. Follow your heart, Maggie. Keep your faith and follow your heart. I know it's a cliché, but that doesn't make it any less true or valid."

Maggie's small smile was genuine. "You make everything sound easy."

"Not easy, but worthwhile. C'mon, let's see what the peanut gallery is up to."

In the living room Tessa had on the radio, and she and Danny and Ian were staring at it, as if their eyesight could help them hear through the static more effectively.

". . . no letup in sight. In fact, the storm actually seems to be intensifying. The temperature is nineteen degrees below zero, but that figure is meaningless because the windchill can approach fifty below in open places. Power is gone throughout the storm area, and crews can't get on the road to begin repairs. The cell telephone transmission tower went down yesterday, so it's not your phone that's dead, it's the system. Please, folks—don't even think about attempting to go anywhere in any type of vehicle, including snowmobiles. This storm is a killer such as Montana hasn't seen in many decades. Again, stay where you are. Do not attempt to—"

"Better turn it off, Tess," Danny said. "We don't want to run down the batteries."

Maggie picked up the blanket she'd been using on the couch and dragged it to the wall adjacent to the fireplace. "What time is it?" she said. "It feels like we've been here forever."

Ian tilted his wrist toward the fire and read his watch. "Twenty to eleven. I guess we all ought to think about getting some sleep. Maybe tomorrow . . ."

Maggie knew that the words of the radio announcer were too fresh in all their minds to even begin convincing themselves that the next day would be any different.

"We have a couple of air mattresses and more blankets upstairs on the beds. We'll need more wood and we'll need to melt snow for water."

"We won't run short on snow," Ian said. He stood. "Want to haul some more firewood into the basement, Danny?"

"Sure. We might as well stock up for the night up here too, and then the two of us can take turns feeding the fire."

Maggie pushed herself up from the floor. "I'll carry wood with you guys—and I want to be in on tending the fire overnight."

"I'll help too," Sarah said. "Danny's right—we need to bring lots of wood in."

"Sarah," Ian said, "your hands are too important to bang them up hefting logs. When this is over you're going to be needed very badly, and if your hands are stiff or bruised or if you happen to catch some fingers between logs, you'll never forgive yourself."

"I can carry wood! Let's not be ridiculous. There's no reason I can't do my share of the work, and I won't have—"

"Sarah," Danny said sharply, "Ian's exactly right. We can't have you risking hurting yourself."

"What about your hands, then?" Sarah snapped. "Don't your patients count?"

"Hey, ladies and gentlemen," Ian said, stepping between the physician and the veterinarian. "Come on, this is silly. Danny wrestles with horses and cows and dogs and all sorts of potentially dangerous critters every day, Sarah. He's not going to get hurt, and he's a lot stronger than you are."

"Not when she's angry, I'm not." Danny grinned.

"You keep that in mind, Dr. Pulver," Sarah said, also smiling.

"It was the Monopoly game," Tessa said. "You're all testy because I whipped you so badly."

"That must be it," Maggie added.

She was about to say something else when the tree limb exploded through the living room window, spraying the area with shards of glass. The wind struck the fire like a gigantic fist, and spewed embers and bits of burning log onto the couch, the carpet, everywhere. Maggie screamed and spun away from the fireplace, slapping at the back of her head, her palm stinging as it crushed the ember lodged in her hair. Tessa screamed too and beat at her face and chest with her hand. Sarah moved to help Tessa, pulling the girl to the floor and whacking at her with both hands. Danny grabbed the edge of the coffee table and flipped it in front of the fireplace, trying to block the wind to the now-roaring fireplace. "Get the embers out!" he shouted. "We gotta get all . . ." The last of his words were lost to the wind.

Ian ran for the two buckets of melted snow in the bathroom upstairs. He stumbled on the first stair and went down hard but was up and scrambling in a heartbeat.

Maggie stomped on the embers on the rug, smashing them out, the bottoms of her feet screaming in pain. She wasn't sure where her boots were, and there was no time to look for them. Panic formed images of the Morrison home burning, driving them out into the storm, where they wouldn't last more than a couple of hours.

Ian bolted into the living room with a bucket in each hand.

"Here, Ian!" Danny shouted. "The couch—put the couch out!"

Ian dumped the first bucket at the end of the sofa, where the fabric and stuffing were engulfed in flames. Danny yanked a burning cushion and, staggering against the force of the wind, stumbled to the gaping window and hurled it out into the storm.

Tessa and Sarah pounded and stomped at burning spots on the carpet, using their feet and their hands.

"Danny," Ian shouted over the wind, "we gotta block that window."

"A table," Danny answered. "We need another table to nail over it. We gotta do that from outside or the wind will blow it off. Sarah, do you have a hammer and some nails? Another table larger than the window?"

Sarah smashed out another burning spot and yelled, "Hammer and stuff is in the basement. There's an old dining room table down there with magazines and papers piled on it. Take that."

Danny looked around the living room while Ian grabbed the flashlight from the kitchen. "It looks like we got all the embers," he shouted into Maggie's ear. "Keep looking for new ones and make sure the old ones are out. Ian and I will—"

"Come on, Danny!" Ian called from the kitchen.

Ian was ahead on the basement stairs with the flashlight. He swept the beam around the frigid cellar. Snow was banked against the far wall, carried in through the gaping hole left when the wind had ripped the door off hours earlier. Basic hand tools were arranged neatly on a pegboard above a small workbench. Danny tugged a hammer loose and snatched a handful of nails from an open box on the bench. The nails were sizable; the groundskeeper had been using them to repair a storage shed.

Ian's light found the table, which was covered with magazines, newspapers, advertising circulars, and various junk mail. He swept the surface bare with a swing of his arm. Danny wrenched the table over onto the pile of paper. "We gotta get the legs off—this thing will weigh a ton, and it'll be hard enough to carry in the wind, even without the legs."

The table was old and of the thick, stable, post-WWII design. Danny stood back a step and kicked out at the table with the bottom of his foot. The leg creaked and tilted. The next kick sent it skidding across the floor. Ian attacked the leg closest to him.

"Maggie eased down the basement stairs in the semi-darkness, clutching an armful of coats and boots. "Everything's out upstairs," she said. "Let's get dressed and get outside. The living room's like a hurricane."

Ian covered the pile of clothing with the light, and the three of them grabbed at coats, boots, and gloves. In moments, they were dressed.

"Hey," Ian said. "Maggie, you don't need to—"

"Stop. Just stop. It's going to take three of us to control this thing outside."

Danny and Ian's eyes met. "She's right," Danny said.

They hefted at the tabletop—now legless—and grunted at its weight as they rested it on an edge and then picked it up. Danny led the way to the door and the few cement stairs to the outside, Maggie at the middle of the table and Ian at the end.

"Keep it as close to the house as you can," Ian hollered. "We'll have better control."

The storm struck them like a knockout punch, and the broad table acted almost as a sail, seeking to wrench itself out of their hands. Visibility was perhaps a foot, and often less than that. The crystalline snow lashed their faces and swirled in crazed patterns around them. They dragged and carried the tabletop along the foundation of the house, following the shape of the home to the battered-in window.

Danny put a handful of nails into his mouth, with the ends jutting out from between his lips. Ian and Maggie crouched, got firm holds on the end of the table, and slid it up the wall, covering the shattered window and its frame. Danny swung the hammer hard, but the wind kept upsetting his aim so that at times he would hit the nails off center and splay them sideways, and at other times miss them completely. After an eternity, they managed to secure the table.

"Ian, can you give me a boost? I gotta get the top of this thing nailed in."

Ian formed a U with his hands, and Danny put a boot in his friend's hands and hefted himself upward. Ten nails later the job was done. The trio linked hands and followed the line of the house back to the basement. The flashlight, after being exposed to the power-sapping cold, was dim, its cone of light ineffectual.

Sarah and Tessa had candles going once again and had moved the coffee table away from the front of the fireplace. The fire was regenerating, licking at the fresh wood the women had added. Danny, Maggie, and Ian clumped in and stood soaking up the heat. Tessa stepped toward them, a broad smile on her face. She stopped suddenly and raised her hand to her mouth. "Danny!" she gasped.

"What?" he asked.

Maggie then noticed that his lower jaw was covered with frozen blood, with an inch-long string of frozen blood suspended from the right side of his mouth like a red fang. He raised his hand to his face. "Ouch! What's . . . Oh. I had the nails in my mouth. There was nowhere else to put them. I guess my lips froze to the metal."

"Don't rub or scratch at your lips," Sarah said. "I'll get you a damp washcloth. We want that blood to melt off—not be torn off."

"I did the same kind of thing when I was a kid," Maggie said. "My friend and I decided to kiss our mailbox. Another girl dared us to."

"Marcia Mott and I licked a jungle gym in the second grade. Our teacher had to get us loose," Tessa recalled.

"Mine was the chain of a swing in a playground," Sarah offered.

"I've never done anything foolish or potentially harmful in my life," Ian said. He waited a moment. "Although I did eat a tablespoon of Alpo once. So did my friend Julian Goldstein."

"Ewwwww!" Tessa squealed.

Maggie wrinkled her nose. "Why in the world would anyone . . . ?"

"Had to," Ian answered the unfinished question. "It was the initiation ritual for membership in our Secret Wolf Justice Association."

"How many members?" Maggie asked.

"Well . . . just the two of us, actually. None of the other kids would eat the Alpo."

They settled around the fireplace, sipping at mugs of hot chocolate from the pan at the edge of the fire. The adrenaline rush that had accompanied the tree limb episode had receded, and conversation had dwindled along with it. The storm continued to harass the old house, but the temperature in the living room had risen to a comfortable point. The limb, shoved off against the wall and forgotten, breathed the scent of fresh pine into the room as it thawed.

Sound sleep was hard to find that night. Montana nights were generally profoundly quiet, and the creaking of the Morrison house and the incessant, spirit-chilling assault of the storm were like spikes of pain that brought those who were dozing to rude consciousness. Maggie, wrapped in a luxuriously thick blanket on the floor with a throw cushion from the couch for a pillow, drifted behind her thoughts, touching sleep at times but not really losing herself to it.

When Danny or Ian loaded logs into the fireplace, the

hissing and crunching was like a circus rambling through the room. At one point Danny's voice said, "Ouch, darn it!" when a flame licked his hand.

Maggie smiled. *A big, outdoorsy, muscular guy who spends lots of his time working on the horses and cattle of foul-mouthed cowboys says "Darn it" when he gets burned? What a great man. He cried when Dancer was born. My mom once said that sometimes it takes a very strong man to allow himself to cry.*

Maggie drifted to sleep again. A *snork* that could only be someone battling tears brought her back to the living room. She waited until she heard it again.

"Tessa? What's the matter, honey? We're all going to be OK. There's no reason to cry."

"I'm not crying! I just have . . . a nasal infection or something."

Maggie's heart hurt for a moment. "Yeah. I've had lots of those nasal infections at night lately. For almost a year now." She let a half minute pass. "What's the matter, Tess?"

Tessa tried to control her voice, but it cracked as she spoke. "My Turnip—and Dakota and Happy and Dancer and Dusty—and Sunday, locked in Danny's mudroom. They're waiting for us, and we can't get to them."

Before Maggie could respond, Danny's voice—even though lowered—seemed to fill the room. "There's very little my GMC can't get through, ladies. That's why I bought it. It'll go anywhere through anything. I'll get to my dog tomorrow, and I'll get to the horses."

"But the radio . . ."

"I heard it, Tessa. The same guy who tells me the stuff he

advertises can grow hair on a watermelon told me there's a storm. I'll get through."

"Not alone, you won't," Ian's voice added. "I'm going with you."

Maggie heard a sigh from across the room. "Sure is a lot of testosterone in this old house tonight," Sarah said. "Hush, everyone, and go to sleep. We'll see how things look tomorrow."

There was a long silence. Then Ian growled. In a heartbeat, Danny joined him, slavering and snarling like a bear pulling down prey.

Tessa giggled—and then Maggie and Sarah joined her. Before too long, all of them slept.

Maggie's eyes opened. The light had a graininess to it—the sort of half-light that seems to struggle with the darkness. It was cooler in the room; perhaps the fire needed tending. Outside, the banshee wind howled unabated.

A log collapsed in the fireplace, and the sound caused Tessa to move in her sleep and move a bit under her blanket. After a moment the girl's quiet breathing resumed.

One of the men was snoring lightly, in a slow, somehow comforting rhythm. She thought of the growling, macho posturing of Ian and Danny a few hours before and smiled.

They're both important to me. They're different men—very much separate in their personalities and their approaches to life. Logically, Ian should be the more serious of the two, the one more inside himself, and yet he isn't. And there's a quiet power to Danny and an encompassing love for the creatures he treats and the people with whom he comes in contact.

I care about both of them, Maggie admitted to herself. *I care deeply.*

She recalled one of the few conversations she and Rich had had about the dangers of his work as a test pilot. It was before they were married, when her engagement ring was still a new fixture on her finger.

"I need to say this, honey," he'd said. "If something happens to me, I don't want two lives to end. I don't want to be morbid, but before we marry, I want you to promise me that if I should go down, you'll go on and find a life with someone else. That's the way life is supposed to be."

"Stop, Richie—please stop!" she'd protested. "I couldn't . . . I wouldn't ever . . ."

"Hush, honey—don't cry. I'm not trying to scare you. I'm an excellent pilot, and I've pulled out of bad situations before—flameouts, stuff like that. I lost an engine once, and brought the bird home. I've . . . well . . . there were other bad times, but here I am, right where I belong, with you. But I need you to promise me . . ."

The smell of coffee brewing pulled Maggie out of her memory. To her, the aroma of freshly brewed coffee had more wake-up-and-get-to-the-day power than the most strident of alarm clocks. She unwrapped herself from her blanket, stood, stretched, and rubbed her eyes. The coffeepot was hanging on the rod in the fireplace, the embers just below its bottom a mix of red and dirty white.

"About time," Sarah pointed out, moving from the end of the couch to the fire and filling a mug from the still-bubbling pot. The fire was regenerating, licking at fresh wood that Maggie hadn't heard being placed in the fireplace.

"I thought you'd never get up," Sarah said. She handed the mug to Maggie.

Maggie sipped at her coffee; it was scalding hot and seemed strong enough to melt a steel horseshoe—and tasted simply wonderful. She took a step closer to the doctor. "Is the toilet OK? I'll get some snow, but I need a bucket."

"All set, Maggie. There are a couple of buckets up there, already pretty much full. I woke up early and thought I might as well do something productive. I never realized how much snow it takes to melt down to even a half bucket of water."

"I never really thought about it, either—but I'm glad you did what you did. Very glad." She drank some more coffee. "What's the radio have to say today?"

Sarah's eyes dropped from Maggie's. "Not good at all."

Tessa unwrapped herself from her blanket, stood, and joined her mother and friend.

Maggie looked across the room to where Ian and Danny were standing in front of the largest window. They weren't speaking and, in fact, appeared to be frozen in place, not even lifting the mugs they each held. Maggie felt a quick, sharp pain in the back of her throat. "Maybe . . ."

"No," Tessa said, her voice much older than her years. "No maybes. This is the storm of the century—that's what the National Weather station called it. I heard the broadcast earlier when Ian turned it on." She raised her eyes to meet her friend's. "My Turnip and Danny's Dakota and your Dusty and Happy and your little Dancer—they don't have a chance. Cattle are frozen solid, Maggie. The guy on the Coldwater station said that. He said that way back in the frontier days was the last time there was a storm like this."

"Those cattle are pastured, Tessa, out in the open, not in a good, stout barn or a mudroom that stops the wind and keeps the snow out. The coat on Sunday, honey—that's the best insulation in the world. The animals will be cold, and they'll be hungry and thirsty when we get to them, but they'll be fine. You'll see."

Unless the horses have panicked already and hurt themselves, or broken through their stalls and gotten to the barrels of grain. If they did that, they'd eat until they dropped. It could kill them. And if the temperature is so low that Sunday goes to sleep and freezes to death, coat or no coat . . .

Tessa must have seen fear in Maggie's eyes. The girl turned away, biting her lower lip, and walked toward the kitchen. Sarah began to speak but then remained silent. Maggie glanced over to where Danny and Ian still stood at the window. She and Sarah joined them.

The window was heavily rimmed with frost, but someone had cleared a rough circle about the size of a dinner plate on it. Outside was a gray, whirling miasma of turbulent snow lashed by a wind that was relentless in its cruelty.

Maggie touched the veterinarian's arm. When he turned to her, his face was grim and hard. "No go, at least right now, Maggie," he said. "My truck would take the snow in four-wheel, I'm sure of that. But I wouldn't be able to see a foot in front of me. I wouldn't be able to find the road, much less stay on it. It'd be suicide. I'm sorry."

"You don't have to apologize to us," Sarah said. "There's absolutely nothing you—or any of us—can do." She looked at Maggie and mouthed *Tessa?*

"She's in the kitchen," Maggie said.

"Let's leave her there for a moment," Sarah said. "What about the horses? Danny was saying they could be in trouble."

Maggie shook her head. "They could be. There's no way to know. They're herd animals, and at least they have one another close by. But if one of them started to take down his stall, they'd all follow, because it's their nature to do so. Turnip would probably be the culprit—he's fairly high-strung and a little too smart for his own good. Horses strike out and fight in raw panic. They're out of food and water by now, but horses can survive amazingly long times without food. The water . . . I don't know."

"But your barrels are good," Danny said.

"Right. I bought the safety barrel with the snap-on tops. They can be knocked over without opening. But I don't think the top would stay on one of them if Turnip or Dakota backed up and kicked. If that happened, they'd eat themselves to founder and maybe . . ."

"I know that," Tessa said. "You don't need to keep your voices down." The clamor of the weather and the urgency of the conversation had covered the girl's approach. Now, the four adults looked at each other guiltily, as if they'd been attempting to put something over on Tessa.

The girl managed a smile. "Now, what are we going to do?"

"Nothing we can do right now," Danny said. "As soon as there's the least bit of visibility, I'll be out there four-wheeling. You can bet on that."

"We'll be out there," Ian corrected.

Danny nodded. "Yeah. Sorry, Ian." He turned to Maggie. "I'm going to need a list of what medicines and supplies you have in your barn. And write down what you've been feeding each horse per day—what supplements, vitamins, and so forth. I'll need to—"

"What?" Maggie almost shouted.

Confusion clouded Danny's face. "I just said that I need—"

"If you think for one minute that you're going anywhere near my barn without me, you're out of your mind, Danny Pulver! Where you came up with such a birdbrained idea is beyond me—but I'll tell you this: that truck of yours isn't moving an inch—an inch—without me in it." She drew breath, glaring at Danny. "Is that perfectly, absolutely, positively clear?"

"Wow," Sarah breathed and then began clapping.

Danny blushed like a little boy caught in a fib. "Listen, Maggie," he said. "I . . . uhh . . . Hold on a minute, OK? I didn't mean that your help wouldn't be valuable. I just didn't want you to expose yourself to what's out there."

"I'll expose myself anytime I want to!" Maggie snapped.

There was a beat of silence while what Maggie had just said penetrated the tension. Ian burst out laughing, and after a moment so did Sarah, Tessa, and Danny. Then so did Maggie. "That isn't exactly what I meant," she said lamely.

Danny held up his hands in complete surrender. "OK, OK," he said. "I give up."

"Maggie could be awfully important when you go out there, Danny," Tessa said quite seriously. "Suppose you needed some cookies baked or coffee made and she wasn't there? Then what?"

"Or," Sarah added, "something crocheted or knitted?"

"Come on," Danny pleaded. "I already gave up. Gimme a break, here!"

Time had a sludge-like quality that day. A Monopoly game failed to hold the group's interest, as did Trivial Pursuit. The men were antsy and frustrated, spending much of their time looking out the window and pacing about the frigid house aimlessly. Ian spent an hour or so with the Morrison family Bible, and the group started a good discussion on Scripture, but the moaning of the house and the constant haranguing of the wind broke into comments and thoughts.

When Sarah switched on the radio the group gathered around her where she sat on the couch in front of the fireplace.

". . . disaster area by the governor at 1:00 p.m. today, and we're right in the middle of it, folks. The National Weather Bureau says the winds have abated slightly, but you sure couldn't prove that here in Coldwater. I just looked out the studio window here on Main Street, and the visibility is hovering right around zero feet, and that wind is howling like a mama bear. Windchill right here in town is minus forty-three degrees—that's killing weather, ladies and gentlemen. Snowfall is guesstimated at about four feet, but I don't know how they figured that—the stuff doesn't sit still long enough to settle in that wind. Remember, no travel of any kind, including snowmobiles. I'll be right here with you, friends, until we can see the sky again. Keep your dial set at . . ."

Sarah turned off the radio. "Well," she said. "The word *abated* sounded awfully good to me."

"Me too," Danny agreed. "Maybe by morning things will have calmed down enough for us to get out."

"I'm going to make some hot cocoa to celebrate," Tessa said.

"Easy, honey," Sarah cautioned. "We don't know that there's any reason to celebrate quite yet."

"Sure we do, Mom. You heard the radio."

"You know," Maggie said with a smile, "I think Tessa is right. Maybe we were too quick with our doom and gloom."

"Maybe so," Ian agreed. "Right now, I'm feeling better about a Monopoly game to go with that cocoa. Anyone else?"

It was a long game, but Tessa won again.

There was no actual dawn to watch Saturday morning. Instead, the more profound darkness of deep night slowly gave way to a half-light that accomplished nothing but to allow Maggie, standing at the window, to see how hopeless any sort of attempt at travel would be. The screech of the wind grated in her ears and on her nerves like the tines of a fork being dragged across the surface of a dinner plate.

Ian joined Maggie at the window, his hands around a coffee mug. Frigid air from a moments-ago wood-restocking foray surrounded him like a cocoon. Maggie shivered. "No change out there?"

"No. If anything, I think it's even colder. Danny says the wind is stronger. That's the way it felt to me too."

Maggie sighed. "I was just thinking how it'd be if I hadn't come here Thursday. I had the line already strung to the barn, so I'd be able to take care of the horses—if I could hang on to the line."

"It's good that you're here, Maggie. But, no matter what, I wouldn't have let you be alone. I'd have gotten to you as soon as this mess started. I mean that. I wouldn't have let you be alone." His fingertips, warmed by the coffee mug, very gently touched Maggie's hand, lingered for a heartbeat, and then moved away. Maggie closed her eyes, and for a bit of time the storm and her fear for her horses were swept away by the intimacy of the moment, by the warmth of Ian's touch.

The clatter of a pot or pan to the floor in the kitchen

shattered the moment. The weather—and the fear—rushed back to destroy the iota of respite Maggie had found.

During that third day of the storm, it seemed as if time, like everything else in and around Coldwater, Montana, was frozen solid. There was little conversation in the group, and no laughter and none of the customary teasing. Tessa, curled up at the end of the couch, stared into the fire. Sarah, next to her daughter, held a medical journal open in her hands, but her eyes didn't follow the copy and she hadn't turned a page since she'd opened the publication. Danny stood at the window silently, as unmoving as a statue. Ian, deep in his own thoughts, sat in front of the fire, staring at nothing. Maggie sat wrapped in her blanket to the side of the fireplace and dozed.

Images of Dancer in his stall taunted her. The colt was the most vulnerable of the horses. His young system could least handle an overload of grain, and if they'd all smashed out of their stalls and the geldings began fighting, he could get between them and be injured. Even Dusty, if caught up in rage or panic . . .

Sweet Dusty. Her temperament alone was worth a million dollars. She was such a gentle-natured horse. Richie had learned to ride on her, and she was the best teacher in the world. She hadn't gotten angry once when he'd accidentally yanked on her mouth or miscued her. Maggie was the one who'd gotten mad—shouted, "Keep out of her mouth, Richie!" The look he'd given her—like she'd discovered him whipping Dusty or something—had made her feel awful for yelling at him.

"You OK?" Danny's hand was on her shoulder. "I thought you might be having a bad dream. Maggie? You were—"

"No. I'm . . . yeah. Just a bad dream is all."

"Dreaming about the horses? Me too. But Sunday, mostly. He's been—he is—a great dog. I've never seen another like him."

Maggie nodded. "Sunday's the best. When you're out riding he sticks close to me, following me around, watching me do my chores or whatever it is I'm doing. And it's not because he's looking for a Milk-Bone, either. We've become awfully good friends."

The veterinarian swallowed hard before he spoke, and Maggie heard the quiver in his voice. "That's what he is to me too. I don't think humans really own dogs like Sunday, any more than parents own their children. We share our lives with them, and they share theirs with us." His hand, still resting on Maggie's shoulder, closed lightly and then moved away. "I better get some wood in," he said. He turned from her, but not before she saw the glisten of tears in his eyes reflected in the candlelight.

For some reason, sleep came easily to Maggie that night. It was as if she slipped away from the storm and the house and drifted, warm and free and secure, in a world where no horses and no dogs were trapped or frightened. The next thing Maggie knew, a hand was gently pushing at her arm. Then Tessa's voice said, "Come on, Maggie—the weather's better. Danny says it's time to go."

8

Maggie tugged on a pair of Tessa's snow pants over her jeans. Sarah's woolen socks made her feet feel cramped in her boots, but she knew she'd need the extra warmth. The loose fisherman-style sweater she wore over the snugger, standard-sized sweater—both of which Tessa had provided—made upper-body movement difficult. That effect was multiplied when she struggled into her own sheepskin coat. She trudged to the window, clutching the mug of coffee Tessa had brought to her.

A lunar landscape had replaced the Morrison yard, outbuildings, and the Montana countryside. The wind, greatly diminished, nevertheless continued to snipe at and sculpt the snow. The morning light was a washed-out gray filtered through the still-falling snow. Despite the heavy clothes, she shivered briefly. She finished her coffee and carried the mug to the kitchen, where the others were gathered.

"I've got a couple of things to say before we go out," Danny said, "but here's what we all need to keep in our minds every second we're outside: don't, for any reason, run or exert yourself so that you have to draw deep breath. The radio said the temperature is right around twenty-five to thirty below. Sucking in that air will burn your lungs—mess them up for the rest of your life."

"Breathe through your noses," Sarah added. "That'll warm the air slightly before it reaches your chest. Keep scarves over your mouths and noses. And keep your heads covered—it'll conserve body heat."

"I'm pretty confident my truck will go over or through anything in our way," Danny said, "but if it gets hung up somehow, we can't spend time or energy wrestling with it. We have to start walking back here right away—slowly. OK?"

"One thing I have to tell you now," Maggie said. "If we make it to my place, I won't be coming back here. Until the storm is over and the temperature rises, I'm going to have to walk the horses in the barn—keep them moving as much as possible to keep their body temperatures as safe as I can."

"I thought about that," Danny said. "I'll stay with the horses. After we get Sunday, you and Ian drop me at your place and go on back here."

Maggie shook her head. "That won't work. Neither Ian nor I can handle that four-wheeler the way you can. We'd never make it."

"Suppose I stay with Maggie and you come back here, Danny? That would—"

"No," Danny said quickly. A surprised silence followed. Danny lowered his voice, face flushing. "What I meant was that we all . . . I don't know," he concluded lamely. "Look—the storm isn't over. The Weather Bureau said it could go another two full days."

"I won't negotiate on this," Maggie said. "There's food and a big fire all laid out in my fireplace. I have lots of wood a few feet from my back door. I've already run a line between my house and the barn. I have candles and a good radio. The horses need me, and I'm going to stay with them." She added, "I'll be just as well off there as I'd be here, except solo Monopoly isn't much fun."

Tessa took a step to the side to face the others. "I'll go with you, Maggie. If you're going to be walking the horses, you need help. There are five of them and one of you, and Dancer doesn't lead terribly well."

"Oh, honey, you can't—" Maggie began.

"No, Tess," Sarah said, interrupting Maggie.

Tessa's eyes narrowed, and her face became hard. Her voice was flinty, with a tone in it Maggie had never before heard from the girl.

"I don't need two arms to lead a horse or a couple of horses up and down an aisle in a barn," she said. "We're not talking about hanging wallpaper here. I can do this—and I will do this."

After a moment, Ian broke an uncomfortable silence. "Actually, Tessa makes good sense. She'll be in no more danger at Maggie's place than she would be here, and she's right about the horses. If they need to be led up and down, it's at least a two-person job, right? The aisle isn't wide enough for someone to walk more than two horses, and that'd mean the others would be in their stalls."

"Yeah," Danny said. "But you're assuming we'll get to Maggie's. I don't doubt that Tess and Maggie will do fine once they're there. We have absolutely no guarantee that'll happen. Suppose we get stuck or I go off the road and can't get the truck out? What then?"

"As you said earlier—we walk back here," Tessa said. "Slowly, breathing through our noses."

"But Sarah will be here alone," Maggie said.

"We brought in enough wood for a full day and a half—maybe two days," Ian said. "Sarah would be in no more danger alone than if all of us were here."

All eyes swung to Sarah. Maggie noticed fear in her friend's eyes for the first time since the whole horrid episode had begun.

Sarah sighed. "Go get dressed, honey. Grab a couple of my sweaters and a pair of my jeans to go over yours. Grab one of those big mittens of mine with the fur inside. And please, honey . . ."

"I'll be careful, Mom. We all will. I promise." Tessa turned to leave the kitchen, but Ian's voice stopped her.

"We forgot something," he said. He looked from face to face. "Let's pray."

They stood outside the back door in a knot for a long moment, easing the transition from warmth and safety to a desolate and hostile tundra. They stood close to one another through instinct, like young children huddling together in the face of danger. The wind swept about them, jagged-edged and biting, flapping loose ends of scarves, finding and numbing exposed flesh.

Maggie's truck, now a mound of snow, stood a couple of feet behind the back of Danny's truck, another mound. The separate garage that housed Sarah's Rolls was covered by a towering wave of snow. Ian's compact car looked enough like a Hostess Sno Ball that the image appeared in each of their minds. "Makes me want a glass of milk," Ian observed.

They moved forward, snow squeaking under their boots as if they were stepping on very vocal mice. The depth varied according to the whimsy of the wind and the storm—in places a yard deep and tightly packed, in others a foot of softly granular accumulation that offered almost no resistance to their strides.

Maggie's truck, doorless on the driver's side, was solidly packed with snow.

"How are you going to get out, Danny?" Tessa asked. "There's no room to maneuver."

"I'll push Maggie's rig out of the way—it should move fairly easily on the snow."

"If your truck starts," Ian worried aloud.

"It better. I paid a hundred and twenty dollars for a heavy-duty battery. Let's clear my windows as well as we can. Remember—work and move slowly."

Danny pressed a small red button on his key case. The chirp and click of the doors unlocking was all but lost to the weather. "Electronic entry," he said, smiling. "Guaranteed not to freeze."

"Is this a General Motors infomercial?" Maggie asked.

"Order up some hot chocolate from your onboard Snack Facility, Danny," Ian suggested. "Then let's see what's on TV in your optional GMC Family Recreation Center."

"I want to spend a little time in the available-at-extra-cost-from-your-dealer Teen Fun Arcade. Wanna play some video games, Maggie?" Tessa said, tucking her head close to her friend's to be heard.

Maggie laughed, just as her three friends did. But the laughter had an artificial quality to it, one that pulled a phrase her father often used into her mind: whistling in the graveyard at midnight.

Danny opened the driver's door, and Ian stood in front of it, using his body weight to keep it from being wrenched off by the wind. The veterinarian tried to slide the key into the ignition and then eased the key back out and put it into his mouth. "Moisture frozen in the cylinder," he said. After an interminable few minutes, he tried the fit again, this time exerting more pressure. The key mated. He turned it. The starter motor complained for several seconds, sounding ready to surrender to the cold—and then the big V-8 fired, stuttered for a heartbeat, and boomed into life.

Danny sat tensely at the wheel, his toe playing with the gas pedal, teasing the engine until the idle found its rhythm and became smooth. He attempted to engage the four-wheel-drive lever and found that the shift lever felt like it was encased in cement. "Let's finish getting the snow off the windows," Danny said. "The truck has to run awhile and warm the gear lubricant before I can do anything with it."

The engine chugged on, like a strong horse carrying a beloved rider where it was necessary to go. Danny had the defrost fan blasting at its highest speed, and it began erasing the thick crust of ice from the windshield. After a dozen or so minutes, fingers of actual heat began to blow through the vents, stroking the stinging faces of the four people who'd clambered into the vehicle.

Danny tried the floor-mounted shift lever. There was a slight clash from under the rig as he found reverse. He moved the stick back to neutral. "Few more minutes is all," he said. "No sense jamming gears when a little time will let them work like they should."

Maggie, in the front passenger bucket, watched Danny's face closely as he watched his dashboard gauges, unaware of her scrutiny. He touched the shift lever again with his fingertips, moved it the slightest bit, and then withdrew his hand.

He's even kind to machines. It's not that he's afraid it'll stall now—he simply doesn't want to ask too much from it, to hurt it.

Danny revved the engine and slid the gearshift into reverse. He released the clutch in increments, easing his foot upward very slowly. The knobby tires chewed snow for a few seconds and then found purchase. There was a light thud as the rear bumper tagged the front bumper of Maggie's truck. Then Danny's vehicle began to move backward, with

Maggie's truck sliding over the ice and snow like a sled. Danny flipped on the emergency rack lights over the cab and swung away from Maggie's Ford like a majestic cruise ship leaving behind a tugboat.

"Wow," Tessa breathed.

"You betcha, girl," Danny said with a grin.

The truck crept forward at a couple of miles per hour. The tires argued for traction every so often, and the chunky treads bit through inches of ice and smoked for moments until they hit the concrete of the driveway and then caught, hurling the truck forward, parting drifts higher than the vehicle itself.

"This thing is amazing," Ian admitted.

Danny didn't respond. He squinted through the curtains of snow, tense, at times biting his lower lip. His left hand had a death grip on the steering wheel; his right hovered over the console of shift levers next to him. "There's a wire down here," he said. "See it, there to the right? I don't know which way the pole fell. We don't want to get hung up on it if it's across the road."

The truck stopped so suddenly that all of the passengers slammed into their shoulder harnesses. "There's that pole," Danny said. He shifted to reverse, backed a few feet, and fed gas to the engine. The tires squealed as the truck rammed forward—and then they felt another impact, and the truck stopped, just as suddenly as it had a moment before.

Danny touched a toggle switch set into the dash near the shift levers. "This is kinda illegal," he said. "It cuts out the entire exhaust and catalytic converter systems and gives me a bunch more horsepower. Remember the old Corvettes with the outside pipes? It's the same idea. Hold on."

The engine escalated from its grumble to a feral roar, and the truck surged ahead, tires screaming. Danny wrestled the steering wheel when the impact took place, and then they were over the downed pole, again plowing through huge drifts of snow.

Maggie reached over to Danny and put her mittened hand on his arm. "Whadda guy," she said, and she wasn't at all sure that she was joking.

The power poles were the only reference points they had as to orientation on the road. On all sides of them was an endless, pale tableau that was frightening in its utter sameness, its lack of landmarks or detail. The truck crunched, plowed, and forced its way ahead at little better than walking speed. The heater began to channel more warmth, and the crusted ice began to melt on the inside of the windows.

"There's Sheïla Ingram's farm," Maggie said. "That means we're a bit more than halfway to my place." A surge of excitement—of anticipation—struck her. "We're going to make it—we're really going to make it!" Her optimism spread to the others as infectiously as a giggle in a kindergarten class. Danny grinned with his friends.

Ian leaned toward Maggie from the seat directly behind her. "This is all going to work out fine, Maggie. I know it is."

Danny shifted into second gear and applied power. "Maggie's farm comin' up," he shouted. For the briefest bit of a second the wind parted the snow like a curtain, and Maggie's house appeared a quarter mile ahead, standing forlornly in a desert of white. Danny powered around a drift that was much taller than his truck and shifted back into first gear. The curtain closed as quickly as it had opened, but the peek at one of their goals filled the truck with urgency.

Maggie's driveway was impassable. A long, seemingly meandering shelf of snow perhaps nine or ten feet high ran most of its length. Danny wheeled toward the front lawn, the rain gully between the road and the grass giving the truck a brief battle. He swung wide of the house, the side of which was banked with snow to the second-story windows. The barn hulked ahead, but very little of it was visible from the front; the accumulated snow was easily ten feet high at the large front door.

"Back door, Danny—it's out of the wind. Or you can leave the truck here."

Danny's response was to step on the gas pedal. The GMC's tires churned and the rig lumbered ahead, hugging the side of the barn. When he shut down the engine, the whining of the wind was almost quiet by contrast. Everyone was out in a moment, with their scarves tugged over their faces as they scrambled to the barn. The slight grade leading to the rear door for drainage had become an apron of glare ice covered by a couple of feet of snow. Maggie was the first down when her boots found no purchase on the ice. Since she was protected by layers of clothing and the soft texture of the snow, the impact felt much like falling onto a featherbed. Tessa's feet flipped out in front of her, and she landed on her seat, whooshing snow into the air as she laughed. Danny did his best to drag Tessa back to her feet, but he crashed down next to her.

A long, raspy squeal—a sound that conveyed excruciating pain—stopped each of them. Maggie lurched to her feet, half falling again, and slammed into the sliding door. She jammed her shoulder against the door to break it loose from the ice in its track. In a heartbeat Danny and Ian were beside her, and then Tessa. They heaved against the door, and it begrudgingly began to slide open.

The murky light in the barn presented a spectacle that made Maggie's heart stop and her mind cease to function. Dusty and Dakota stood with their heads down, eating high-protein sweet feed from a fifty-gallon drum on its side toward the front of the barn. The drum's safety lid was creased and battered and sitting against a wall. Maggie could see that it had been torn off by the repeated kicks of shod hooves. A couple of bales of hay Maggie had brought down from the second level three days before were scattered about, as if shaken violently by a giant hand. Dakota's stall door, its center splintered and sagging loosely on its hinges, gaped like an open cave. Happy stood facing Dancer's stall, her eyes pleading, her muzzle spattered with blood. Turnip's stall gate was smashed open as well—Maggie gasped as she saw the battered and broken boards, a crushed and twisted grain trough, and grotesque splatters of frozen blood appearing as black as India ink about the stall.

But none of that clutched at Maggie's heart like the spindly hind leg of a colt protruding through a jagged hole in the stall from which the horrible cry of pain was keening.

The leg was twisted and cut by the splintered wood, and the hoof hung at an impossible angle. Blood dripped steadily from a shard of the cannon bone—the longest bone in the hind leg of a horse—where it had pierced Dancer's skin.

Danny shoved past Maggie and shouted over his shoulder, "Ian, Tessa, somebody! Get my bag—hurry! Maggie, we don't have time for you to stand there. Move! Come on, I need your help!"

Maggie broke from her semi-trance like a swimmer emerging from a deep dive, dazed for a second but already in motion.

Danny crouched at Dancer's stall and tore away the scraps and spearlike projections of broken wood that held the colt's lower leg trapped. Ian thumped the medical bag down next to Danny. Maggie reached over and opened the latches.

"Ian, see what I'm doing here?" Danny said. "I'm going to move back for a minute, but I want you to keep easing this leg free. Tessa, if there's room, you slide in next to Ian. And look, folks—no matter what you do, you're going to hurt Dancer. There's no way around it. We don't have much time to play with here. Get that leg free."

Dancer, still on the other side of the stall gate from the humans, squealed as Ian peeled part of a board from under the damaged leg. Tessa drew in a breath sharply but made no other sound as she slid a jagged sliver out of the young horse's flesh.

"I'm going to do some suturing, Maggie," Danny said, his hands filling a large hypodermic, "and I need you to swab and watch for bleeders. The cannon bone is snapped, and as soon as we get the area clean, we'll splint it and then I'll go to my place—I've got a Fiberglas casting kit there."

"Almost clear," Ian said. "There!"

Tessa climbed over the gate and into the stall and held Dancer's leg as Ian eased the gate open. Danny was there with his hypodermic, sliding the tip skillfully into a vein. Dancer, eyes ringed in white, chest frothy with frozen sweat, snorted loudly and began to cry out again. Then his head slumped to the hay-littered floor and he was still.

"Oh no!" Tessa shrieked. "Dancer . . ."

"He isn't dead," Danny grunted. "The anesthetic dropped him. He's out of pain now. You get those horses away from the sweet feed, Tessa. Whack 'em if you have to, but get them away from there. And cross-tie Dusty in a stall. She's driving me nuts dancing around here." He met Maggie's eyes. "Set yourself up next to me, Maggie. Wash your hands with the bottle of alcohol from my bag—it's the best we can do right now. Leave enough for me."

"I'm going for the cast kit and Sunday," Ian said.

Maggie looked up at him. "But you don't—"

"I watched every move Danny made from Sarah's house to here. I can drive the truck. OK, Dan?"

"Go," the veterinarian said, clattering surgical instruments into a small metal pan and waiting for Maggie to hand him the alcohol bottle. "There are a couple of good flashlights in the mudroom cupboard. Bring those. You can't miss the casting kit—it's in the same cupboard and it's the size of a suitcase and says Equi-Cast on the front of it. I just got it a few days ago—I haven't even unpacked it."

"Tess," Maggie said, "get the flashlight from the shelf by the saddles. This light is awful."

The growl of Danny's truck sounded from outside. After a moment of idling, the tires whined and engine racket built up as Ian tickled the accelerator and began rolling—hard and fast. "He'll make it," Danny said.

Danny worked quietly, his lips moving silently every so often as he debrided the break and maneuvered the lengths of bone together. Tessa held the light on Dancer's extended right rear limb as steadily as a beacon.

"Maggie," Danny said after a long forty-five minutes, "the plastic box with the stainless steel screws in it in my bag—open it and hold it in front of me. It's the—"

"I've got it, Danny. There's a seal—"

"Yeah. It's sterile. Pull the tape all the way around the container and—"

"Here, Danny."

"Good."

The first screw—the big one—went in easily. As Danny turned the setting tool, the trimmed and prepared lengths of bone drew together as if pulled by a gentle and benign magnet. The second screw—the one to mate the fracture closer to the hoof—began to slip. "Push against what I'm doing for a second, Maggie. All I need is the slightest bit of grab here. Easy, honey—there . . . good. Real good."

It was finished.

The tagging of flesh together with sutures was a first-year vet school exercise. Danny fell back from the hunched position he'd held for the last hour and more and blinked rapidly, his eyes as fatigued as his hands. "Whew," he grunted.

Maggie leaned over Danny, her hand, now trembling, moving a sweaty hank of hair from his forehead. She kissed him, her lips barely touching his; the sweet contact was almost frightening in its intensity. She moved her mouth a part of an inch from his. "Thank you, Danny," she breathed. "Thank you for what you've done for Dancer and for who you are."

"Whoa," Tessa murmured as she led Dakota and Turnip on short lines past Dancer's stall.

Maggie and Danny blushed instantaneously and in perfect unison said, "Tessa . . ."

"I know, I know," the girl said. "I didn't see a thing, but even if I had, I'd never tell anyone. OK?" She turned the two horses and led them toward the front of the barn.

The reverberation of Danny's truck and, a moment later, a series of frantic barking broke the moment. Suddenly, Sunday was running full-tilt at Danny, throwing himself at his friend, now whining rather than barking, his tail whipping, his tongue lapping at Danny's face. Danny hugged the big dog to him like he would a beloved child.

Ian set the casting kit on the floor and lowered a twenty-five-pound bag of Gravy Train dog food next to it. "I didn't want to take the time to feed Sunday, so I brought his grub with me." He grinned. "If all those I visit at their homes were as happy to see me as Sunday was, I could help save the entire world."

Tessa and Ian built a fire in the house as Maggie and

Danny worked at the delicate process of layering strips of fiber tape the length of Dancer's left hind leg and applying the fixing and setting chemicals to the tape. The vet's heavy-duty electric lanterns provided harsh but more than adequate light. Happy, Dakota, Turnip, and Dusty looked on from their stalls, where they were haltered and secured with lead ropes. Thus far, none had shown signs of founder or stomach distress. When Tessa righted the breached barrel she found that only a few pounds of the protein-rich feed had been consumed—the animals had gotten to the grain not long before their rescuers arrived. The nicks, scrapes, and cuts were relatively minor; Tessa quite competently treated them with a disinfectant wash and a layer of pasty bovine bag balm, referred to by horsemen as the "universal cure for horsehide."

Maggie hunkered next to Danny as he crouched next to the fractured leg. His hands moved quickly but not hurriedly as he smoothed the cast, applied fixer, and frequently checked the colt's pulse and breathing. His concentration was as focused as any surgeon working in a fully equipped operating theater, his moves sure, without wasted motion.

The extreme cold seemed to have little effect on the chemical reactions and the bonding of the casting materials.

"His eyelids are fluttering a little," Maggie said.

"Yeah. I noticed some increase in his pulse too. He's coming out of the anesthesia. That's good—we're almost done here."

"Is he going to be in much pain?"

Danny hesitated. "Some. Maybe a lot. The screws and this cast need to support weight as soon as he wakes up and we help him to his feet. It's instinct—he'll need to stand as soon as he's conscious. There aren't many animals that are easier kills for predators than a horse off his feet, and Dancer's blood will tell him that loud and clear."

"What's . . . what's the prognosis, Danny? I need to know."

Danny shook his head. "I honestly don't know. He's an extravagantly healthy colt with excellent bone structure and lots of spirit. It's completely possible the bone will mend perfectly." After a moment, he added, "And it's completely possible that it may not too. I think his chances are real good, Maggie, but it's out of our hands from here on in."

Maggie nodded. A wave of fatigue rolled over her that made her suddenly, unexpectedly weary. Her balance tottered for a moment, and she put out a hand to maintain her position sitting on her boot heels.

Danny went back to work, smoothing the cast, his fingers probing the edges that were close to flesh for roughness. Maggie watched him work.

I kissed this man who isn't Richie. That moment wasn't only gratitude, and it wasn't merely a gesture. I kissed him as I used to kiss Richie, to show him that I . . . No!

She'd never feel about another man as she did about Rich Locke. Never. But was her kissing Danny only gratitude, then? Why did it feel so good and safe and wonderful? And why, when they were kissing, did Ian's face flash in her mind?

Two hours later a truly miserable colt stood in his stall, leaning slightly against a side wall with the toe of his left rear hoof testing the ground very tentatively. When he shifted weight to the limb he squealed in pain and snatched the hoof up again. Tremors ran through his body every so often, and his eyes were red rimmed.

"The shivers and the red-eye are from the anesthetic wearing off," Danny said. "He's doing fine. He'll put more weight on the leg as he goes along."

"He doesn't look fine, though," Maggie said.

"No," Danny agreed. "But neither would you if you'd just broken your leg and had surgery in a drafty barn by flashlight in the middle of the storm of the century. I think he's going to be OK."

Ian reached over and gently smoothed Dancer's forelock. "He's a gutsy little guy, isn't he? He has to be hurting badly, but he hangs in there. He trusts you, Maggie, and it looks like he's wondering why you don't fix him up immediately—make everything better right now."

Maggie sighed. "I know exactly what you mean. Even with a very young child, a parent can explain that the pain will go away. With a horse . . ."

The windows along the side of the barn clattered in a gust, and a wooden roof truss groaned.

"All we can do is the best we can do," Danny said. "I've certainly learned that in my practice. I wish I could stop all the pain and fear of the animals I treat, but that's not possible. I do the best I can."

"What I know about horses wouldn't fill an ant's hat," Ian said, "but I know a good doctor when I see one."

Danny's face showed quick surprise at the minister's comment, but then he smiled. "Thanks, Ian."

"What about Dusty and Happy and Dakota and Turnip, Dan?" Ian asked. "Is that grain they got into going to be a problem?"

Danny grinned. "Nah—they didn't have enough time with the barrel open to eat themselves sick. As my gastroenterology professor in vet school told me, there's something you can always count on when it comes to horses eating what they shouldn't: 'This too shall pass.'"

Maggie didn't sleep that night. She spent most of her time standing next to Dancer, scratching his ears and neck and comforting him with her words. She dashed to the house every couple of hours and stood in front of the fireplace to thaw her feet and hands and drink large mugs of coffee. Tessa, cocooned in a blanket, slept peacefully on the couch, which they'd dragged closer to the fire. Ian and Danny had set out for Sarah's home shortly before midnight when the wind began to diminish.

It had been an impossibly long and arduous day, and Maggie felt limp with fatigue. Yet, for whatever reason, her mind was flitting from thought to thought and image to image.

Why in the world did I see Ian in my mind when Danny

kissed me? What do I really know about Ian Lane? Ellie certainly likes and respects him, and that's a strong recommendation. I like him too. He brings something with him wherever he goes—something that's uniquely Ian. His sense of humor is wonderful, but there's more. His eyes tell more of a story than his words do—at least about his past. The death of his wife must have been as devastating on him as Richie's death has been on me. Is this a misery-loves-company kind of connection?

"No," Maggie snorted aloud.

Then what was it? There was a lot to the man that she didn't think any of them had discovered. He had a presence to him, not because he was a minister but because of his attitude about life. He'd seen pain, and he'd come out on the other side of it, if not unscathed, then at least unbroken. And he was so interested in everything—so curious. Maggie sensed that he wanted to know people well, to be emotionally intimate with them. He cared about what people said to him as much—or more—than about what he said to them. And he seemed vulnerable too. He seemed like the type who could have his heart torn out by misplaced trust or spurned love. Maybe that was why she found herself being so careful around him, why she sometimes avoided his eyes or stepped away when she thought he was going to say something about how he felt about her. But, for that matter, was she even sure that he *did* have any feelings for her?

At about 4:00 a.m., Maggie sat on a hay bale that she'd dragged into Dancer's stall. The colt's eyes had finally closed.

His right side was to the stall wall and his left rear hoof rested on the floor lightly but, even so, carried some of his weight.

Dancer's eyelids quavered for a second when what sounded like a locomotive climbing a steep grade labored by on the road outside. Maggie hurried to a front window in the barn and stared through the still-falling and swirling snow.

A line of red flashing lights atop what appeared to be a charging leviathan lumbered past, launching massive sheets of snow toward the shoulder of the road. The Coldwater Department of Roads and Snow Control was out and battling the more than five feet of snow that had fallen.

As Maggie walked back to Dancer's stall, her legs trembled. The ache in her shoulders was now a persistent, nagging pain. Her mouth tasted of too much black coffee, and her stomach craved a decent meal—she'd had next to no food since she and the others had arrived at her farm that morning.

Dancer's eyes had popped open at the roar and clatter of the snowplow, and now he stood awkwardly with most of his weight carried by his three good legs. As Maggie watched, he eased the hoof of the casted leg to the floor. His eyes widened at the jolt of pain he must have felt, but he kept the hoof where it was, its surface flat on the floor.

"Brave boy. Brave Dancer," Maggie said, stroking his muzzle. The colt found the pocket of Maggie's open jacket as she hugged his neck and nuzzled inside of it, seeking a treat.

"Tomorrow, Dancer. Tomorrow you can have all the snacks you want," she whispered.

When the roar of the truck was gone into the night, the silence seemed louder than the diesel engine had a few moments ago. The wind was a whimper—and barely that.

The storm had been reduced to an inconvenience rather than a death threat. The sky cleared quickly, and the tormented and churning clouds that had caused all the problems began slinking away like petty thieves frightened by light.

It was over. The storm was over.

9

The Montana winter lumbered on like a powerful but subdued beast of burden.

With it came Christmas, a season of tears for Maggie Locke. The decorations in the windows of the stores in town, the almost omnipresent sound of Christmas carols and songs, the cheery greeting cards, all prodded painfully at Maggie.

It had been hard to tell her parents she wouldn't see them this Christmas—but it had been necessary. Maggie knew that she'd be unable to carry on a charade of good cheer, and that she'd only step on the holiday for her mother and father. They'd understood, and if for nothing else this yuletide season, Maggie was grateful for that.

She attended the early service on Christmas Day, doing her best to force smiles at friends who greeted her but twisting a tissue to damp shreds as she sat as far back from the front as she could.

She slid out of the pew a few moments into Ian's sermon and literally ran to her truck in the overfilled parking lot, sobbing and gasping. The hefty *thunk* of the new door on her pickup as she slammed it closed made her wish that the door could protect her from her heart the way it protected her from the subzero temperature and the gusting wind outside the vehicle.

Danny's truck turned into Maggie's driveway about midday, and she watched it from her bedroom window. She stood to the side so that she wouldn't appear in the frame if the vet should glance up toward her room. Moments later she heard a bark and then a light tapping at her kitchen door.

I could say I was asleep—that I took a sleeping pill. But this has to be hard for Danny, coming here today, particularly after I scurried out of church like such a coward this morning. He means well—I know that. And he genuinely cares about me.

She walked from the window, stopped in front of her dresser mirror, and sighed as she looked at her image. Her eyes were red rimmed and her face blotchy. She'd been clutching a pillow—Richie's pillow—over her head, and her hair showed it.

The tapping sounded again, this time a bit louder. Maggie ran her hands through her hair, squared her shoulders, and headed for the stairs to the kitchen.

Danny smiled when she opened the door. Sunday shoved past him and danced around Maggie; his tail swiped rapidly as he whined and patted at her legs with his forepaws. She crouched to greet the collie, and he lapped at her face, ecstatic at seeing his friend.

"I won't say Merry Christmas, Maggie, but I had to see you today—at least for a minute."

Maggie stood, one hand still scratching between Sunday's ears. "It's OK," she said. "I'll make some coffee. Take off your coat and sit down." She noticed an oversized green envelope that Danny was clutching with both hands.

Maggie gave Sunday a pair of Milk-Bones and measured coffee into her pot as Danny took off his coat and sat at the kitchen table, still grasping the green envelope. Maggie turned from the stove. "What's that?" she asked, nodding toward the envelope.

"It's . . . well, it's a little gift. It's just something I wanted you to have. C'mon, sit down and open it."

Maggie pulled out a chair and sat. Danny handed over the envelope. She took it from him, noted that "Maggie" was written on the front, and then tore open the glued flap. Inside was a pair of pages neatly taped together at the centers. The pages were taken from a farm implement catalog and showed a picture of an Allis-Chalmers Deluxe Small Ranch Manure Spreader.

Danny spoke rapidly, almost tripping over his words. "I got a real deal on a used one, Maggie. A customer owned it, and then his daughter got married and sold her horse. It's in great shape, and yours is about shot. This one will be perfect." He paused for a moment. "Umm . . . do you like it? It'll be delivered tomorrow."

Maggie looked up from the pages. "You . . . you got me a manure spreader for Christmas?"

"Well . . . yeah," the vet admitted, his eyes beginning to show uncertainty. "I thought you'd like it."

Maggie hadn't laughed—really laughed, with the wonderful release that comes with such a moment—in days. She jammed her chair back and hustled to hug Danny, almost taking both of them to the floor. "I love it, Danny! I absolutely love it!" She laughed into his shoulder and neck, not unaware of the scent of his shampoo and the strength of his arms holding her in an awkward embrace. There was no thought to the kiss that followed, no careful alignment of faces, no tentative move that preceded it.

I'm safe in this guy's arms. What could be more delightful than a man who gives a girl a manure spreader for Christmas?

She allowed the kiss to linger for a moment and then eased to her feet. The laughter caught her again, and this time it infected Danny. It was a good moment, and a warm one.

"I have something for you too," Maggie said, going to the dining room table. She picked up a greeting card–sized envelope and handed it to Danny. "I'll warn you, though; it isn't as glamorous as what you gave me."

Danny opened the envelope and removed a twenty-dollar gift certificate in his name to Karen Campbell's Books, the Coldwater bookstore. "This is great," he said. "Thanks, Maggie."

Maggie smiled. "It isn't much." *There's another envelope just like yours with Ian's name on it. And a pair more for Sarah and Tessa.* Maggie cringed inwardly as Danny turned the certificate in his hands. *These people deserve personal gifts—things*

I've picked out for them, things that will mean something to them. She sighed.

"What's the matter?"

Maggie shook her head, not trusting her voice.

"Very dumb question," Danny said quietly. "Sorry."

Maggie swallowed hard a couple of times, avoiding Danny's eyes. "I need some rest, Dan. OK?"

Danny stood. "Sure. I'm going to look in on Dancer. I'll call tomorrow." He walked to her chair and put his hand on her shoulder. He began to lean forward toward her but stopped. Instead of a kiss, he squeezed her shoulder gently. Then, in a moment, he was gone, Sunday at his heels.

Silence settled into the kitchen. Maggie sipped at her now-tepid coffee. The sun streaming in through the window onto the table brightened and then dimmed as clouds scudded past in the blue depths of the sky. Maggie's home felt good to her at this moment—as if its furniture and scents and sounds were embracing her.

Sell out and get out, get away from all this—that's how she'd felt a year ago today. Cut and run. But that wouldn't have made Rich any less dead—and that was the final truth of it. There was good here, and safety, and she was just beginning to believe that again.

She picked up the pages from the farm implements catalog and looked at the pictures, noting that Danny had used scissors or a razor blade to cut the page rather than simply ripping it out, as perhaps 99 percent of males on earth would have done. The farmer on the tractor hauling the manure spreader was dressed like a model from a Land's End catalog. He was wearing gloves, she noticed. His hat was a perfectly creased Stetson, unmarked by sweat, weather, or animal excrement. And behind him, his farm was an Eden, with small groups of perfect trees and fencing that was more precise and straight than any real fence could ever possibly be. Although there were broad pastures beyond the tractor and spreader, there was no sign of livestock of any kind.

It started as a giggle but soon escalated to the free and joyful laughter Maggie had enjoyed a short time earlier. This time, however, there was no one to share it with, and she keenly felt that difference.

Ian crunched and slid up the driveway in his little car just before dark that Christmas Day. Maggie wasn't surprised; she'd expected him earlier, given how she'd fled his service at church that morning. She walked from the couch in the living room to the kitchen door to greet the minister and grinned when, instead of his smile, all she saw through the kitchen window was his back as he walked toward the barn. She flipped on the outdoor light switch and went back to her couch, knowing it would be awhile before Ian appeared at her door.

Love at first sight, Maggie mused. *A minister and a quarter horse colt.*

Maggie sat for a few moments and then rose and tugged her coat from the closet. Snow squeaked under her soles as she walked to the barn, the pristine, arctic air a tonic that awakened her senses. She stopped for a moment and looked up at the sky. The profound and inestimable depth of the darkness would have been frightening if not for the stars in boundless clusters.

A shooting star darted from east to west, its tail glinting like the trail of a Fourth of July sparkler. Maggie watched it, took another deep draught of air, and entered the barn.

Dancer stood outside his stall, quite proudly wearing a white leather halter with brass fittings. Ian, standing next to the colt with his back to Maggie, rested both hands on Dancer's back. Maggie heard the final words of the man's prayer.

". . . your creatures—your creations, Lord. Again I thank you for giving us Dancer, and I pray that you continue his recovery and mend his leg so that he's once again as close to perfect as an animal can be. Thank you, Lord. Amen."

"Amen," Maggie echoed. She moved to him and hugged him lightly. "Good to see you," she said. "I'm sorry about this morning. Things just kind of caught up to me. I shouldn't have . . ."

The young minister held Maggie for a moment or so longer than was necessary. "I understand, Maggie," he said into her hair. "I'm glad you showed up at all." She felt his lips touch the side of her head in a gentle kiss. When they separated, Maggie's hand trailed down Ian's arm, ending with their two hands together.

Maggie nodded to the halter and lead. "Show tack? You

shouldn't have, Ian—he'll outgrow the halter in six months. But it's beautiful."

"I suppose he will. But he'll have it for six months anyway, right? And look, I think he really likes it."

"Of course he does! How could he not?" She eased her hand out of Ian's and crouched at Dancer's left rear leg, running her fingers up and down its length, checking for cracks. She noticed that only the toe of his hoof was touching the barn floor. "Still not putting much weight on it," she said.

"Yeah," Ian agreed. "But I caught him sleeping when I came in, and he was standing on all four, comfortable as can be."

Maggie stood and took a step to the front of the colt. "Danny says it shouldn't be hurting him much at this point. Those bones begin to knit quickly. Part of Dancer not putting full weight on the leg is ghost pain. It hurt him a whole lot once, and in his mind, nothing's changed. When he forgets about it—like when he's sleeping—is when he puts weight on it. He'll be less and less conscious of it as time goes on."

"I . . . suppose," Ian said dubiously.

"No?"

"Well, I read this article in *Western Horseman* about a fellow with an Appy colt about Dancer's age. The writer said—"

Maggie couldn't stop a quick laugh of amazement. "*Western Horseman*? Appy? Ian, you're becoming a cowboy!"

"Shucks, ma'am," Ian drawled. "I reckon I am. Ain't nothin' wrong with that, is there?"

Maggie laughed again. "*Western Horseman* is the best hard-core horse magazine in the world. I had no idea you read it."

"Yup. Got me one of them there subscriptions," he continued in his acutely phony drawl.

"Oh, cut it out!" Maggie laughed. "You'll never sound like a saddle tramp, Ian. But you've really gotten interested in this stuff, haven't you?"

"I have." He stroked Dancer's muzzle. "Look at his eyes. How could a person not love a creature with eyes like that?"

At that moment, Maggie was more interested in Ian's eyes than those of the colt. A quick shiver ran through her—a tiny electrical buzz—that at least for the moment chased away the sad and lonely parts of the day.

How in the world can this be? A little while ago I was kissing another man, and at this moment, my cute minister is making me feel like a fourteen-year-old high school girl infatuated with her teacher.

Ian stopped speaking in midsentence, the moment capturing him just as it had Maggie. They moved together as inevitably as morning dew appears on pasture grass, and their kiss was warm and long. Dancer snorted wetly, demanding to be the center of attention again, and Maggie and Ian stepped back from one another without embarrassment or self-consciousness.

"Well," Maggie breathed.

"Indeed." Ian's voice was raspy, quiet, almost a whisper.

Maggie couldn't control her smile. "Cowboys don't say 'indeed,' Ian."

"Umm . . . shucks all git-out?"

Although they were a stride apart, their eyes remained together, peering inside one another's hearts. Maggie moved to him again, as if eased into the step by a gentle hand at her back.

"Say 'indeed' whenever you want," she murmured. Dancer snorted more insistently this time. The couple ignored him for a long, wonderful moment.

Maggie sat at her kitchen table listening to Ian's car pull down the drive and onto the road. She fingered the Christmas gift he had given her—a delicate silver bracelet—and turned it in the light so that the segments of turquoise shimmered and gleamed.

Everything is different now, and everything is so complicated and confusing, and instead of my husband I have two very good men wanting me, and I don't know if I want either of them—or maybe I want them both.

Maggie set the bracelet on top of the manure spreader pages and walked into the living room, not bothering with a light. She sat on the couch and put her head back, suddenly weary. Moonlight filtered through high, wispy clouds and created stark shadows in the room. The fireplace needed another log, but Maggie was too tired to attend to it. She swung her legs up onto the couch and settled into it.

She felt herself drift off to that strange aspect of sleep in which she knew she was dreaming but yet felt a reality, an immediacy to the dream that made it seem as if it was really happening.

I miss you terribly, Richie.

"I know that, honey. But you're doing the right things. I'm proud of you. I mean that."

I thought I'd die after you . . .

"After I died? Don't be afraid to say it, honey. My life on earth ended a year ago. I'm in heaven now, and I'll be here forever. But you still have a life to live on earth."

Why haven't you come to me before, Richie? I've needed you so much. If you'd come to me earlier—like this—things would be different.

"I can't meddle in your life, honey. But I want you to know that I don't want you to spend the rest of your years on earth alone. Your heart is too big not to share, Maggie. You shared it with me when I was with you, and now you need to share it with another."

It's so soon, Richie—only a year.

"Time is nothing. It means nothing. Let your heart guide you. I love you, Maggie, and I want very much to see you happy again. I know it seems strange to you, but that's the truth and that's what's in my heart for you."

Richie . . . please . . .

"Danny and Ian are both fine men. Follow your heart, honey."

The ring of the telephone sawed through the dream, chasing it from Maggie's now-awake mind. The phone rang three times more, and then the *click-clunk* of Maggie's answering machine picked up.

"Hi, this is Maggie Locke. I can't come to the phone right now, but if you'll leave your name and number I'll get back to you as soon as I can. Thanks." There was another click, a beep, and then Maggie heard her mother's voice.

"Hi, sweetie. You're probably out in the barn, so Dad and I will call again. We tried earlier, but you were out, and you know how your father is about talking to machines. We're having a quiet day. The three of us will celebrate Christmas later in the year, maybe on Dad's birthday, just like we discussed. It's difficult not seeing you, honey, but maybe for right now, we did the right thing. Our hearts are together, anyway. Well, the reason why I'm calling is I want to tell you this: I was half asleep a moment ago, and I had the strangest dream. And somehow, I woke up with the conviction that you're OK, that you will be OK. Mother's intuition? The Lord's intercession? I don't pretend to know. It doesn't really matter, though—because I know what I know. OK, I'm babbling here. We'll try you a little later. We love you, Maggie."

New Year's Eve wasn't a big deal to Maggie, Sarah, Danny, Ian, or even Tessa. The gathering at the Morrisons' home that night was casual—good food, lots of conversation and laughter, and good friends.

"Sorry, Maggie," Tessa said as she scooped up the paltry house Maggie had on Ventnor Avenue on the Monopoly board.

"You're insufferable, you little brat," Maggie pointed out.

"Yep," Tessa agreed.

Maggie felt Danny's hand tapping against her knee under Sarah's kitchen table. She looked down and saw that he was offering her a five hundred dollar bill. She reached down casually and accepted it. "Although I think you forgot that I had this behind me, hidden away right here for an emergency."

"Mom," Tessa said. "Maggie's cheating with Danny. He's passing her money again."

"Danny?" Sarah asked.

Danny blushed. "It's not what it seems, Sarah. Don't listen to Tessa. Maggie and I had an agreement—what's called a depository note in lieu of something or other. We just—"

"Sure, Doctor," Sarah grinned. "One thousand dollar fine. And, you collect nothing if this innocent little kid lands on your properties for the next two turns."

"Innocent?" Danny cried. "Tessa bought up all the junk property and used it to leverage—"

"Hush," Sarah interrupted. "Apparently you've forgotten that I'm the banker and the official arbitrator. Maybe you'd like another thousand tacked on to your fine?"

Ian, the first to be bankrupted by Tessa, shoved his chair back and stood. "I can't be a party to this any longer," he said grimly. "That . . . that twerp drove me to the poorhouse."

"I offered you a loan, Ian," Tessa said sweetly.

"Sure. Just like a great white shark offers a tuna an invitation to dinner. Anyway," he added, "I want to see the crowd in Times Square."

"I'd pay not to be there tonight," Sarah said. "Really. The

racket, the drunks, the pickpockets, the hookers—I don't understand the attraction."

"I was there once," Ian said. "I was a kid—maybe twenty or so, still an undergrad. What I remember of Times Square the most is the smell—the stink. A lady in a fancy ball gown tripped and fell right in front of me, and I grabbed her arm to help her up. *She* was a man in a dress, and another guy in a dress whacked me, and . . . well . . . that was it for me and New Year's Eve in Times Square."

"What were you doing in New York City?" Tessa asked.

"I was working as trim carpenter outside of Albany during the vacation. A friend's father got me the job. The money was good, and I liked the work. It was pretty much hammering nails and helping the real carpenters—the finish guys. I was the one they sent for coffee and sandwiches. Anyway, I had a couple of days off, so I thought I'd go to the city for New Year's Eve, just to see what it was all about."

"You went alone?" Tessa asked.

"Yeah. It was kind of a spur-of-the-moment idea."

Tessa seemed fascinated. "Tell me more about it. It must've been exciting. I've never even been near a crowd of people like that."

"If you're anything like me, Tessa, I hope you never are. It wasn't exciting—it was frightening." He paused for a moment. "Huge crowds like that don't seem right to me. It's like the lowest common denominator takes over. The noise is awful, and the alleged 'fun' seems like some sort of forced . . . I don't know . . . just on the verge of violent mass insanity."

A long silence followed. Finally, Sarah spoke up. "Enough of this grimness. This is supposed to be a celebration, people. Let's lighten up a bit, OK? Let's play 'If I Could.'"

"Mom," Tessa protested, "that's a kid's game. It's dopey."

"Dopey or not—what is it?" Danny asked.

"Tessa's right," Sarah said. "It's a kid's game, but it's fun. Each person tells what he or she would do or see or experience or own if there were no boundaries of any kind at all—time, place, money, whatever. It's a statement of what would make the speaker most happy."

"Not so childish at all," Ian observed. "Let's do it."

"Tessa, you go first," Sarah said.

The girl considered her words for a full minute as she munched popcorn from the bowl on the coffee table. "OK," she said. "What would make me most happy is pretty much what I have now. I thought about going back in time to Woodstock to hear all that great music, and then I thought maybe I'd say I'd like my arm back. But the thing is, what I have right here with my mom and my friends and Turnip is about as good as it gets." She paused and then concluded with a slightly embarrassed, "Ya know?"

"Wow," Ian breathed. "Our little girl's all grown up."

"Your turn, Danny," Sarah said.

Danny spoke seriously. "I flashed on some fancy stuff before Tessa gave us her 'If I Could.' I thought about a huge Olympic-sized swimming pool—indoor—so I could swim all year round. And a Porsche 912. But those things are toys. I have one dream or goal or whatever one cares to call it, but I'm afraid that one isn't for publication." His face colored slightly. "Anyway, I'd have to go along with my friend Tessa. What I have right now is pretty good."

"Maggie?" Sarah said.

"I guess there's no big secret to what time I'd go back to and whom I'd be with, but I don't want to say that. Ian's right; Tess made me see just how very good all of us have things. Danny's right too—all the things that came to my mind were toys. I dunno—I guess in the real world I wouldn't change much." Maggie smiled at her hostess. "What about you, Sarah?"

Sarah grinned. "Essentially ditto. And that's the point of the game. Ian, what about you?"

"If I could . . ." Ian said, "I'd be a father of a child. I don't care if it's a boy or a girl or how many legs or arms it has or what color his or her skin is. It seems to me that the most splendid thing a Christian—or any person—can do is to raise and love and play with and enjoy a child, and get the child started on the right path in life."

Tessa nodded her head. "Cool."

"Quit hogging the popcorn," Ian said. "Pass the bowl, Tess."

Danny smiled. "It's ten after midnight. We missed the ball coming down in Times Square."

"We didn't miss a thing," Maggie said.

"No," Tessa agreed. "We didn't. I think we even gained something." She looked up at Ian shyly and said, "Do you think we could pray?"

Maggie reached for the girl and drew her closer. "If I ever have a daughter, I'd want her to be like you, Tessa," she whispered.

Tessa hugged her. "Maybe one day—no, for sure, Maggie—you'll have a . . ."

Maggie's embrace stifled the girl's words, but Maggie was sure that there was no one present at the Morrison home who didn't realize what those words would have been.

Maggie steered carefully over the patches of black ice that appeared on the road between her home and the Morrisons', snug in the cab of her pickup. Danny had gone out to start the truck as Maggie was saying her good-byes, and she was as warm as she'd be if she were sitting on her couch facing the fireplace at her home.

Ian wants to be a father, wants a baby. A child was what came to his mind first if he could choose from anything in the world.

The rear end of the truck skidded sideways slightly, the tires grabbing for traction on the diamond-hard ice. Maggie eased off the accelerator and steered into the direction of the slide, bringing the truck back under control. She looked at the speedometer: she was going twenty-five miles per hour. Without touching the brake she brought her speed to twenty and kept it there.

And Danny—Danny of the manure spreader fame. Danny and Sunday, the dog with a heart bigger than his big, furry body. In her mind she watched the vet working on Dusty the night Dancer was born.

His hands are strong and gentle. I can still see him assisting at the miracle of birth . . . Danny loves me too, just as Ian does.

I must be the luckiest woman in the world—or the saddest, because one of these wonderful men is going to be hurt.

Maggie pulled up close to her barn and turned off her engine. Her land, her buildings, everything around her was a moonscape under the soft light from above. The wood of the big door creaked in protest as she pushed it open, stepped into the barn, and turned on the lights. The scents of good hay, leather, molasses feed, fresh straw, and the fine, natural aroma of curried horses greeted her.

Dusty's head appeared over her stall door, her liquid eyes blinking slowly, looking as dopey as only a suddenly awakened horse can. There was a piece of straw standing almost straight up in her forelock, like a small spire. Dusty nickered warmly, the sound another sweet welcome. Maggie tugged the blade of straw free and rubbed the horse's muzzle with both hands. Dakota's head appeared, and then Turnip's and Happy's. Maggie scratched necks, touched ears, and patted heads as she walked to Dancer's stall.

The colt was facing into a corner, sound asleep. He was standing squarely—each of his hooves in full contact with the barn floor, each carrying all the weight nature intended it to. Maggie opened the gate and eased into Dancer's stall. She stood at his right hip and pushed lightly against his rump. The colt's instinct told him to move away from the slight pressure, and he did so, putting proportionately more weight on his left rear. The leg carried the added weight without a problem.

Dancer snuffled, winked rapidly a few times, and came awake, turning smoothly to face Maggie. "Good boy!" she told him. "What a good, strong boy! We'll get that awful cast off of you real soon, Dancer. I promise."

The colt extended his muzzle toward Maggie, looking for a carrot or a piece of apple. He stopped midmotion, and his eyes became confused. He blinked twice, as if he were pondering a deep secret, and then lifted his left rear hoof from the floor so that its toe barely touched.

"You faker," Maggie laughed, sliding past him on his right side and again applying pressure to his hip. Surprised, Dancer yielded to the push the only way he could—by accepting the weight on his left rear. His eyes opened wide, not in pain but in astonishment, and he swung his head back to gape at his leg. It took a moment for him to understand that he was, once again, carrying his weight as he had before the Thanksgiving storm. He sniffed the cast thoroughly, as if he'd never seen it before, and prodded at it with his nose. For a second his toe came off the floor again, wavered a bit—and then settled back comfortably, as it had been. He rocked his rump a few inches side to side, testing the absence of pain. Then, satisfied, he turned in the stall to face Maggie and again sought a treat.

Maggie's unrestrained whoop startled all the horses and shattered the late-night silence of the barn.

The next hundred and twenty or so days passed as Montana winter months always did, offering a few days of delightfully warm temperatures and the promise that spring would eventually come but then negating those short respites with endless weeks of below-zero temperatures and howling winds.

Now, though, the sun seemed to be flexing its muscles and was cascading Montana not only with brilliant light but also with a modicum of heat. Maggie noticed a valiant little crocus poking its way through the partially frozen soil as she walked to the barn that morning.

Her kitchen—actually quite spacious—felt strangely like an overheated jail cell because of Ian Lane's pacing between the sink and the table.

"Please, Ian," Maggie said, "sit down. You're driving me up a wall. I mean it. Danny knows what he's doing. If he says today's the day, then it is."

"Yeah," Tessa added.

"I'm sorry. I'm a bit nervous is all. I don't do terribly well with medical stuff."

"He's afraid of Danny's saw," Tessa said to Maggie, grinning. "He's afraid the blade will cut into Dancer's leg." She pretended to think for a moment. "'Course, it probably will. But still . . ."

"Tessa," Maggie sighed, "stop your teasing. You're just going to make him worse."

"I'm not afraid of Danny's saw!" Ian said, quite a bit louder than necessary. "I just get a little queasy thinking about the whole thing." After a moment, he added, "I broke my own leg when I was a kid, and I still have nightmares about the surgery and the cast."

"It's not surgery, Ian—it's nowhere near surgery. The blade of the saw doesn't even have regular teeth. It's a kind of vibrating, spinning thingie that sort of chips away at the fiberglass. It's not like a saw for wood."

Tessa's eyes lit up gleefully. "Of course, there's always the danger of—"

"Cut it out!" Maggie demanded.

Ian stopped at the window facing the barn. "There's Danny," he said.

Maggie joined Ian at the window and saw Danny taking a briefcase-sized aluminum case from the back of his SUV. She and Ian and Tessa rushed out to him.

"Big day." Danny smiled and hefted his case. "Let's get to it."

Dancer stood in his stall, his eyelids drooping from the effects of the injection Danny had given him a few minutes ago. "The sound of the saw is awful," Danny said. "That's the only reason I gave him the shot. Right now, Dancer doesn't much care what I do to him."

Maggie led the colt out of his stall and into the aisle, where she cross-tied his head and stood at his shoulder, stroking his neck. Ian watched from a couple of feet behind Danny, swallowing hard every few moments. Tessa crouched next to the vet. Danny switched on what looked like a carpenter's circular saw with a flat-surfaced, toothless blade. The tool hummed quietly until Danny applied the blade to the cast. The screech of the separating fiberglass and the high-pitched whine of the saw combined to form the frightening shriek of a dentist's drill hard at work.

The dry, acrid smell of burning plastic almost instantaneously permeated the air around the horse and the humans. Motes of fiberglass floated upward from where Danny worked, like strands of spiderwebs caught in rays of sunshine. Danny cut downward first, easing the tool in a straight line to the midpoint of the cast. The last part of the procedure took only moments. Danny cut up from the bottom, meeting his first cut. He pried the cast apart and slipped it off. He handed it to Tessa without looking away from Dancer. The colt put weight on his leg immediately.

"Got any coffee, Maggie?" Danny asked.

Ian, white faced with a line of sweat over his upper lip, applauded the veterinarian's work.

10

The annual Spring Festival in Coldwater was, in Maggie's mind, the official end-of-another-winter celebration. Various organizations spent the month or so preceding the event decorating the Coldwater Grange Hall, a large, drafty, clumsy-looking building that dated back to a decade after the end of the Civil War. The structure itself, a grim, two-story brick edifice with all the architectural imagination and grandeur of a shoe box, hulked gracelessly in the middle of a rutted, potholed parking lot. Even the colored streamers and the huge "Spring Festival" banner on the front of Grange Hall couldn't quite eliminate its stodgy image.

Maggie parked and stepped out into the decidedly spring-like air. It was a cool night, but the sky was clear and the moon was a shade away from full, and she was sure that if she had a stepladder, she could reach up and touch the stars that hovered above.

She breathed deeply. The very air promised growth and fertility and early hay and fine, fat cattle and sleek, healthy horses. The ground under Maggie's boots yielded slightly to her weight rather than crunching or snapping as it had for so many winter months, and the sensation was a pleasant one. She avoided the scattered puddles in the parking lot, saving the shine she'd spent an hour polishing into her boots. Further, the hem of her dress hung well below her knees, and splashes of mud would look terrible on the lace. Dress was Western for the Spring Festival, and Maggie, whose usual outfit was jeans and a shirt, felt like a fairy tale princess in her taffeta square-dancing dress with its several petticoats and lace trim.

Maggie noticed Ian's car in the line ahead of her, and as she got closer to it, she stopped and smiled. On the left rear window was a dinner plate–sized decal showing the head of a horse with the legend "The American Quarter Horse: Speed, Style, Heart."

Two figures leaned on the hood of the little car, apparently in deep conversation. Maggie took another stop and saw through the darkness that the two were Ian and Tessa. Maggie raised her hand and began to speak, but Tessa's giggle stopped her.

"This is soooo exciting," the girl said. "But are you sure, Ian? Absolutely, positively sure?"

"Yeah. No doubts at all. If she says yes, I'll be the happiest man in the world. I've thought it all over carefully and prayed about it, and it all feels right." Ian stepped away from his car. "C'mon, Tessa. Let's get back inside. Maggie'll be here soon."

Maggie crouched a bit behind the cab of a pickup, feeling like a sleazy spy for listening in on the conversation. But there was a far stronger and more frightening sensation that made her body tremble.

Ian's going to ask me to marry him. She turned and stumbled back to her truck, this time paying no attention to mud or puddles. Once in the vehicle, her hand, although trembling almost spastically, fit the key into the ignition. She stepped on the clutch—and then released it.

What good will running away do? I need to face this. I need to make a decision, and scurrying away like a schoolgirl won't accomplish a thing. A sob wrenched deep in her throat. *But how can I decide? And what about Danny? If I'd overheard Danny saying the same words, what would my reaction have been?*

Maggie swallowed hard. *The simple fact is that I don't know—I don't know if I want Ian or if I want Danny—or even if I genuinely want either of them in my life full-time right now. If only there were someone to help me with this, someone who could put things in perspective, guide me in making a decision. If only Ellie were still . . .*

Maggie's hand hadn't stopped trembling, but this time she didn't hesitate to turn the key. The engine came to life, and she jammed the floor-mounted shift lever into reverse and tossed pebbles and mud as she wheeled out of the parking space and shot out onto Main Street. The closest telephone was at Hildebrand's Mobile Station only a few blocks away. Her tires chirped as she floored the gas pedal.

The enclosed booth stood under an arc light fifty feet from the series of pumps. The station was dark inside, and the bay doors were snugged down and locked for the night.

Maggie pulled next to the booth and took a handful of change from the glove box. As she did so, a sudden memory flitted into her mind. The day she and Rich had picked up the truck, Rich had put five dollars worth of quarters into the glove box. "For a telephone call or a sandwich or whatever," he'd said. "Who knows what can go wrong—even with a brand-new truck."

Maggie held several of the quarters for a long moment. She took in a deep breath, got out of the truck, and entered the booth, pulling the accordion door closed.

". . . and then they went into the festival, and I went back to my truck and came and called you. Ellie, I don't know what to do."

"Whew. That's a bit of a tough one, honey." She hesitated for a moment. "I . . . well, I need to tell you this. My meds are working fine. Some days I'm a little fuzzy, but most of the time I'm rational and lucid—and that's how I am today."

"I didn't think . . ." Maggie sputtered.

"You called for advice, or at least to talk about a problem, Maggie. You need to know that I'm all here to discuss it with you—because I am."

"Thanks, Ellie," Maggie said quietly.

"Sure, honey. Now, remember the old adage 'Marry in haste and repent in leisure'? I think it's possible to apply that here, isn't it?"

"I . . . I don't know. I guess so, but they're both such great guys, and I . . ."

"It's not both of them whom you think is going to ask you to marry him, Maggie. It's Ian."

"I know."

"You sound like you're a mess, with all your snuffling and gasping. You shouldn't be. You should be proud and happy that such a fine man wants you as his wife."

"But, Ellie—"

"Hush for a moment and hear me out, honey. As I said, you should be pleased and proud. But there's no way in the world you can give Ian or Danny or anybody else on God's green earth an answer tonight—and you're under absolutely no obligation to do so. You need to go to the Lord with this, and however long it takes for you to decide, well, that's how long it takes."

An eighteen-wheeler rumbled by outside the telephone booth, and Maggie didn't answer her friend until the racket of the engine and the shifting of gears had passed.

"Where are you?" Ellie asked. "Sounds like you're on a racetrack or something."

"I'm at the Mobil station on Main Street. Ellie, I get what you're saying. But the truth of it is, I'm not completely sure how I feel about Ian or Danny. I mean . . . I guess I love them each . . . both . . . whatever. But to tell either of them . . ."

"Let's slow down here, honey," Ellie said. "You're going way too fast, and you're making a big assumption that there's no reason for you to make."

"I don't understand. What assumption?"

"You don't owe Ian an answer tonight, or at any time until

you're totally confident in saying yes or no. It's a woman's prerogative. You've got to get that through your head."

"But suppose I tell Ian it's too soon, but Danny hears that he asked me. Danny's such a white knight he's liable to think I'm betrothed just because Ian asked, and I'll lose Danny. See what I mean?"

Ellie's chuckle was rich and warm and comforting. "Of course I do. As I've been trying to tell you, you need some thinking time—whether that time is a day or a month or a year. That's all there is to it."

Maggie sighed. "All there is to it. I wish it was that easy."

"It is, honey," Ellie said. "The Lord has lots of time for you. Go to him. OK?"

"I'll try," Maggie said quietly.

"Good. What are you going to do right now?"

Again, Maggie sighed. "Go home, I guess. I've got—"

"No!" Ellie said. "You're not going home to pine and sigh and carry on like some soap opera star, Maggie Locke! You go back to that festival and you dance and laugh and play those silly games they always have and you let whatever's going to happen with Ian and Danny happen. You hear me, child?"

"I . . . yeah. OK. And Ellie?"

"Hmm?"

"I love you. Thanks. You're great."

Maggie drove back to Grange Hall more calmly—and much more slowly—than she had left it when she'd been seeking the nearest telephone.

Ellie's phrase "a woman's prerogative" floated in her mind.

Of course it's up to me. But I have no obligation to make a decision until I'm completely ready, and that realization makes me feel good—stronger, somehow. Not many of us were made to be alone, and marriage is a fine and godly state of life. I know how very good a true partnership can be. I've already been there with Richie.

She flicked on her turn signal, pulled into the Grange lot, and parked in one of the few remaining spots. Music and laughter from inside the building reached her as soon as she opened the door of her truck. She listened for a moment and then smiled as words of a line carried to her: "Darlin', it's been a cold and lonely winter . . ." Maggie nodded in agreement with the lyrics and started toward the Spring Festival.

The colors and the sounds and scents inside the warehouselike building were almost overpowering. Long, graceful streamers hung from the high roof beams, shifting and twisting above the crowd, their vivid hues a benign cloudburst of color.

Dress was predominantly—in fact, almost exclusively—Western. Creased, new-looking jeans, polished boots, and pearl buttons and snaps were everywhere, as were petticoated square-dance dresses in bright, homey colors. On a small elevated platform toward the rear, a rock group—the Average Garage Band—was finishing the song. Along one side of the room was a series of long tables, each covered with dishes, casseroles, plates, bowls, and trays of food. One table—the one with the youngsters clustered around it—offered cookies, cake, doughnuts, several kinds of pies, tarts, bear claws, and other pastries. Fruit punch, soft drinks, and canned soda covered one table, barely leaving room for the commercial coffee urn.

"Maggie!" Tessa rushed up and embraced her friend. This night, the girl's eyes seemed even more full of happiness than was usual for her. "You're so late—where have you been? Isn't the band great? They're playing lots of real old stuff, the Beatles and the Rolling Stones and Richie Havens."

Danny wove his way through the crowd and smiled at Maggie. "About time you showed up," he said.

"Tessa's filling me in on what ancient music the band's been playing, reminding me how old and decrepit I am."

"I have not! It's just that I've spent half a day with kids in the Saddle Club from school, and I'm sick of boy-band music."

"Not me. I can't get enough of that stuff," Ian said from behind Maggie. He stepped around to her front and smiled. "Good to see you, Maggie." He nodded to Danny and extended his right hand. "Mrs. Nowack tells me you saved her Missy's life again, Dan."

Danny laughed, taking the minister's hand. "I've never seen a dog that eats more junk than Missy does. The last time it was a roadkill squirrel. This time it was three athletic socks."

Tessa tugged at Maggie's arm. "C'mon, let's play some of the games. Ian? Danny? C'mon!"

"Good idea, Tess," Ian said. "And in the spirit of the

Spring Festival, I'll win a teddy bear for both Tessa and Maggie," he added solemnly.

"One teddy bear for both of us—or do we each get one?" Tessa asked.

"Waitaminnit here, Ian," Danny said. "That sounds like a challenge to me. I'm the one who'll win teddy bears for these fine ladies. Choose your game."

"Hoops," Ian said with a grin.

Sarah, almost breathless, joined them as they made their way to the "Two-in-a-Row-Wins-a-Bear!" setup.

"A patient turned sour—sorry I'm late. Have I missed anything?" she asked.

Tessa hugged her mom and began to answer, but Ian spoke first.

"Danny has been foolish enough to challenge me in a game, Sarah. I'm about to win bears for Maggie and Tessa—and one for you too."

"All talk and no action," Danny said.

"Well, let's get to it, then," Sarah said. "I can't stand the tension a minute longer."

The netless hoop was set at about nine feet on a metal pole anchored by sacks of sand. The foul line was ten feet from the pole. A mound of teddy bears rested on a card table to the side. The ball was a thick, ungainly rubber bladder about half filled with water. Ian stood at the foul line, the ball shifting like a living thing in his hands.

"I suspect that this isn't a standard basketball," he announced.

Maggie watched Ian's first attempt wobble through the

air. It sagged and twisted like a ruptured tire and missed both the basket and the pole by a yard.

He lost his wife—and I'm sure that he had with her what I had with Richie. But he went on with life, was open to it, and didn't allow his faith to be shaken. He's a strong man underneath his jokes and his teasing—a man who would cherish a wife, treasure her, share everything with her . . .

Danny stepped up to the foul line. Julie Downs, vice president of the Coldwater chapter of the National Barrel Racing Association and a reporter for the local newspaper, carried the ball to him. She was running the booth and obviously enjoying herself. Julie was very pretty—blond and blue-eyed and as lithe as a Kentucky yearling, with a sense of humor and a positive approach that made her one of the most popular club members.

Julie has her eye on Danny. Then she wondered why the idea irritated her. *Jealousy? No. But still . . .*

Maggie watched as Julie leaned to Danny and whispered something in his ear. When she handed the bladder to him she took a moment to adjust his hands on it and then stepped back.

Maggie's eyes caught Sarah's for a speck of time—just enough for a message to be passed between them. *Sarah picked up on it too. Julie Downs is more interested in Danny than she is in her booth.*

Danny's first toss was, if anything, clumsier and less accurate than Ian's.

He's blushing because he blew that throw so badly. It's really important to him to win a scruffy little teddy bear for me. And that time when he held me and we kissed and I felt so safe, so protected from everything . . .

Twenty minutes and twelve dollars and fifty cents later, Tessa had wandered off to join a bunch of friends who were throwing darts at balloons to win a gigantic stuffed Garfield, and Maggie and Sarah were discussing the weather.

Ian stepped to the line and held the ball, a significant part of it hanging on either side of his hands, not unlike a clutched water balloon. He turned his back on Julie and the goal and stared at Sarah and Maggie until they stopped talking.

"Ladies," he said solemnly, "I'm out of quarters." He sighed dramatically before going on. "Dr. Pulver has beaten me not with his basketball skills but with his bank account!"

The affair wound down not all at once but as couples and families said their good-byes and drifted toward the door. Youngsters and toddlers were sound asleep and carried by their mothers or fathers, and older children walked in the short steps of the overfed, more than a few pasty faced and clutching their stomachs.

With the majority of the revelers gone, the hall took on the look of a vast cavern, in which sounds echoed hollowly and the streamers and decorations seemed to have lost their excitement and joy and become used and forlorn.

Danny, Ian, Sarah, Tessa, Maggie, and a group of others lingered in the hall, stuffing trash cans and sweeping the floors. Out of the corner of her eye, Maggie caught Tessa leaning close to Ian and whispering in his ear. The minister nodded, smiled at the girl, and said something Maggie couldn't hear. A moment later, Ian stood next to her.

"Walk you to your truck, Maggie? I . . . I need to talk with you for a second."

The fun and the laughter of the evening drained away for Maggie. She felt like a captive with nowhere to run.

"Ian," she began.

"It'll only take a minute. Please. I know it's late and you're tired, but this is important. I'll get our coats. OK?"

Maggie nodded, not quite trusting her voice. Danny, she noticed, was looking at some sort of a book Julie was holding. Julie had apparently found some coffee somewhere; each of them held a cup as they talked.

There were perhaps eight or ten trucks and cars still in the Grange Hall parking area. They walked toward Maggie's truck at the periphery of the lot, their boots crunching the now-frozen mud.

"I've been spending a whole lot of time at your place lately, Maggie. I guess you know that."

The words sounded rehearsed and practiced to Maggie, and she didn't doubt that they were. *How can I hurt this sweet, gentle man? And what if I say yes? Would that really be a bad thing? Could I be happy with Ian?*

". . . don't want things for the sake of things. I have my work and my duties here in Coldwater, and . . . well . . . I've become so interested in horses. And Dancer. You know how I feel about him."

They stopped at the driver's door of Maggie's truck, and

she turned to face Ian. Even in the cloud-filtered light, he looked like a nervous schoolboy. "The thing is," he said, "I've thought about this and I've prayed about it, and in my heart I know and believe it's a good thing." He swallowed hard. "So, I'll just ask you." He took her hand and held it, and Maggie felt the dampness of his palm.

"So, I'll just ask you," he repeated. He swallowed again. "Will you sell Dancer to me?"

"What?" The word came out as a startled gasp more than a question.

Ian stood perplexed, mouth slightly open, gawking at Maggie as the laughter rolled—poured—from her.

"Ian . . . Ian . . . you're wonderful!" she choked as she clutched the startled minister in a hug.

"I have the money, and I'd board him at your place and pay you to help me with his training."

Maggie eased away from Ian and leaned against her truck. "I'm sorry, Ian. I just . . . I . . . thought that you . . ."

"I what?" he asked.

"Nothing. Just a silly thought is all."

Ian cleared his throat. "About Dancer . . . ?" he asked.

"We'll work something out, Ian. I promise we will. I know how you feel about him."

"Wonderful!" Ian exclaimed. "That's really great! Hey, let's get a coffee or a Coke or something, OK? I'm too wound up to go home just yet."

"There's nothing open in town, Ian. It's after 11:00."

Ian sighed. "Yeah. I guess you're right. It was a good night, wasn't it? I had a good time at the festival, managed to grind you into selling Dancer to me—or making some kind of arrangement, anyway—and met some people I hadn't yet met."

"You didn't win a teddy bear for me, though," Maggie teased.

"Alas."

Maggie got into her truck, closed the door, lowered the window, and turned her ignition key. "Night, Ian. We'll talk about Dancer real soon."

"Great. Good night—drive carefully." He began to turn away and then turned back. "Hey, who was that lady—Julie? At the basketball game? Seemed to know Danny? I introduced myself to her but never got a chance to talk—seems like her booth was the most popular one of the night."

"Julie Downs. She's a reporter for the *News-Express*." Her next word came unbidden. "Why?"

"No reason," Ian said. "Seems nice is all." He smiled. "Night, Maggie."

She watched Ian as he walked to his car, and then she engaged her clutch and rolled out of the parking lot. "No reason," she said aloud mockingly and squealed her tires as she swung onto the road. "No reason," she repeated in the same mocking, little-girl tone. Then, in a moment, she laughed.

He's a minister! He's supposed to know the people of Coldwater, and particularly those who come to his church. The image of Julie Downs, blond hair swirling, blue eyes sparkling, rolled through Maggie's mind.

She didn't laugh again during her trip home.

11

Sarah Morrison blew across the top of her coffee cup, dissipating the steam, and then took a sip. "Mmmm. That's good coffee, Maggie. But let me get this straight. That was the night of the Spring Festival, correct? Almost five months ago?"

"Right. I drove on home and went up to my room. I was tired and confused, but I still had the feeling that had come to me in my truck. I was distraught—at least a bit—but there was a difference. I wasn't scared any longer, Sarah. That's the thing: the fear had dropped away. I picked up my Bible that night and I read it for maybe a half hour. I hadn't done that for a long time. It felt good."

"Good in what sense? I'm not sure I understand. Was there some sort of revelation?"

"No, it wasn't like that. I suppose this sounds silly, but the image and sensation that immediately comes to mind is this. When I was in the third grade, there were a couple of girls who picked on me all the time. I'm not even sure why they did, but they did. One rainy day those girls and a couple of boys were giving me a tough time after school, calling me names and splashing puddles at me and nonsense like that. I lived about a half mile from the school and walked both ways. I was soaked from the splashing and the rain, and the wind was cold, and I was completely miserable, feeling totally alone and unloved—and then I got home. I opened the door. My mom had been baking, and I smelled peanut butter cookies and felt the warmth of our house. My mom came from the kitchen and hugged me even though I was dripping wet. She got me out of my wet things and into fresh clothes, and we had cookies and milk together. I've never forgotten how good that time was. And that's what I felt like when I turned out my reading lamp that night of the Spring Festival."

A shriek from outside broke into the conversation in Maggie's kitchen. Sarah rushed to the window. After a moment she said, "Come look at this."

Maggie joined her friend at the window and watched as Danny focused the hose he'd been washing Dakota with on Tessa as she ran around the paddock, trying to avoid the ice-cold stream of water.

"I'm certain Tessa did nothing to prod Danny into spraying her," Maggie said.

"Absolutely," Sarah agreed. "The girl is without fault in all things."

As they returned to the table, Tessa shrieked again. Maggie topped off their coffee cups before she sat down.

"We—all of us—noticed the change in you," Sarah said. "But in a sense, it was subtle too. You were different. Lighter,

I guess, more open. Less trapped inside yourself. It was good to see."

They sat in the late August sun cascading through the window, quietly, companionably, enjoying each other's company. Hoofbeats sounded from outside, and Maggie went again to the window. Tessa and Danny were mounted, headed up a grade in the pasture outside the training paddock, both as comfortable in the saddle as working cowhands. Their horses were in a gallop, reaching out with their front hooves and dragging ground beneath them, tails streaming like banners. Dancer ran the fence line of his own pasture and pushed hard to maintain the couple of strides he was ahead of the other two horses.

"They look like a postcard from a dude ranch, don't they?" Sarah said as she walked over to join Maggie. When Danny and Tessa topped the rise and rode out of sight and Dancer had gone back to grazing, Sarah faced her friend.

"You've done wonderful things in the past few months. You've made a perfect decision and you've . . . I don't know . . . come back to planet Earth, I guess."

Maggie looked down and stared into her coffee cup.

"He's happy for you, Maggie," Sarah said quietly. "He told me that he is, and I believe him."

Maggie nodded and then raised her head to meet her friend's eyes. "I hope so," she said.

Sarah smiled and went on. "I don't know if you realize it, but Tessa has learned so much from you. She's learned about love and pain and life choices and recovery from loss.

She loves you to pieces and respects you more than I can begin to tell you."

Maggie blushed, and both women laughed. "How could I not love that girl like I do, Sarah? God doesn't make many like her. She's a gift and a blessing."

Sarah smiled. "I talked to her again about a prosthesis. I told you how she said she'd rather have her stump than some phony plastic thing everyone would gawk at. Well, I've been bringing catalogs home from the hospital. Some—many—of the devices aren't half bad, you know. The articulated ones look almost natural, and all kinds of progress has been made in prosthetic science—really amazing stuff." She sighed, but the smile remained on her face. "It's up to Tessa, of course. Anyway, she said she was going to talk with you about it, and I wanted you to be prepared." She laughed. "That's not precisely what she said—she said she'd ask you if you thought she'd look good with a silver hook, like the pirate in Peter Pan."

Maggie laughed. "Like I said, the girl's a blessing, Sarah—to all of us."

Sarah glanced at her watch. "Whew! I've got to run. Big day tomorrow, and I've still got some things to do. And I promised Tessa I'd pick up a new pair of jeans for her."

"The new surgeon—what's his name?—is working out well?"

"Steve Ridley. Yeah. He's excellent. Nice guy too—a little arrogant, but a nice guy. The nurses flock around him like bees to honey." Sarah moved toward the door. "How do you think Tessa will do tomorrow?"

"Well, Turnip's ready. He's been burning up the pattern and leaving the barrels standing up. Tessa might be pushing too hard for that extra half second she can save by jamming the barrels too closely. If she keeps cool, she'll do real well."

"Thanks to your training."

Maggie laughed. "Nah. Tessa belongs on a fast horse. She's a natural. I've guided her a bit, but all the raw talent was there before I met her, before I had anything to do with her riding."

"I guess we'll see tomorrow."

"We sure will. And even if she takes down all three barrels and runs over a judge, she's still our Tessa."

That evening, when the sun had lost its power for the day but was still providing gentle, dusky light, Maggie left the barn and walked the fence line of Dancer's pasture. The other horses were in their stalls, but Dancer needed all the exercise he could get, and his evening meal was scheduled later than those of his barn mates to give him as much time as possible outside.

Maggie stopped and whistled a short note—and then immediately grimaced as Dancer wheeled his body toward the sound and placed much of his weight on his left rear leg as he turned. *Nothing to worry about*, she chided herself. *Danny says he's as fit as he was before Thanksgiving.*

Dancer, gregarious as ever, galloped across the pasture to where Maggie stood, sliding to a decidedly show-offish stop.

Maggie started toward the barn, and the colt, on his side of the fence, tagged along after her like a puppy, snorting every so often as if to hurry her somewhat unhurried pace to the feed barrels.

Maggie saw Ian in her mind as she walked, remembered him sacking Dancer—rubbing the colt's body with an empty grain sack, beginning to flap it gently around the horse's neck and face to acclimate him to the hurried moves of humans. Dancer had been clearly bored by the process. *It's going wonderfully—perfectly. They're learning at the same time. The bond between Ian and Dancer is . . . is like a partnership—or a good marriage. There's so much for each of them to learn, but they have all the time and space and love they need.*

Maggie stood outside Dancer's stall, listening to him grind sweet feed between his teeth and the occasional grunt that indicated his joy at eating. After a minute, she picked a handful of carrots from the treat basket and went stall to stall to give each horse a carrot, a scratch between the ears, and a few low words of love.

As she walked toward her house after securing the barn for the night, she stopped midway. The light in the second bedroom—the office—was on. Maggie took a deep breath of air that smelled of fresh grass and the humid sweetness of a Montana summer night. *This is all good.*

Maggie continued on into the house, leaving her boots on the mat in the kitchen. She started up to the second floor, her thick socks quiet on the stairs.

Ian was hunched over the keyboard, unaware of her presence in the doorway as he worked on the coming Sunday's sermon. He was a good typist and a quick thinker and writer. Maggie focused on the cadence of his fingers as they tapped out letters, words, sentences. The simple gold wedding band on his left ring finger that matched the one Maggie now wore and had barely become accustomed to glinted as it caught the light from the desk lamp.

This tiny moment in time, Maggie somehow knew, was a picture of joy and love that would be in her mind and her heart forever.

"Hey," she said quietly. "I've been standing here watching you work."

Ian leaned back in his chair and turned toward her. "That doesn't sound terribly interesting for you."

"It all depends on one's perspective," Maggie said, moving to embrace her husband. "I find it fascinating."

A Note on Barrel Racing

Barrel racing is a fast, hard-riding, intensely exciting sport that pits women and tautly muscled, precisely trained horses against a merciless and unforgiving clock. Since its inception in the 1940s, barrel racing has become a favored event in the Professional Rodeo Association's shows and competitions, and a woman with a strong and competitive horse and a whole lot of personal grit and determination can earn prize money that rivals that of male calf ropers and rough stock riders.

The sport works like this: three empty polystyrene fifty-five-gallon drums are set in an arena. The distance between the barrels varies, but the rules call for a minimum of one hundred feet and can go longer, depending on the size of the arena. A safety zone is provided to allow the contestants to slow and stop their mounts, which are galloping at top speed after completing what is called the cloverleaf pattern. Although the majority of riders opt to take the righthand turn first (since most horses turn more strongly to their left), taking the left barrel first is allowed. The pattern looks like this:

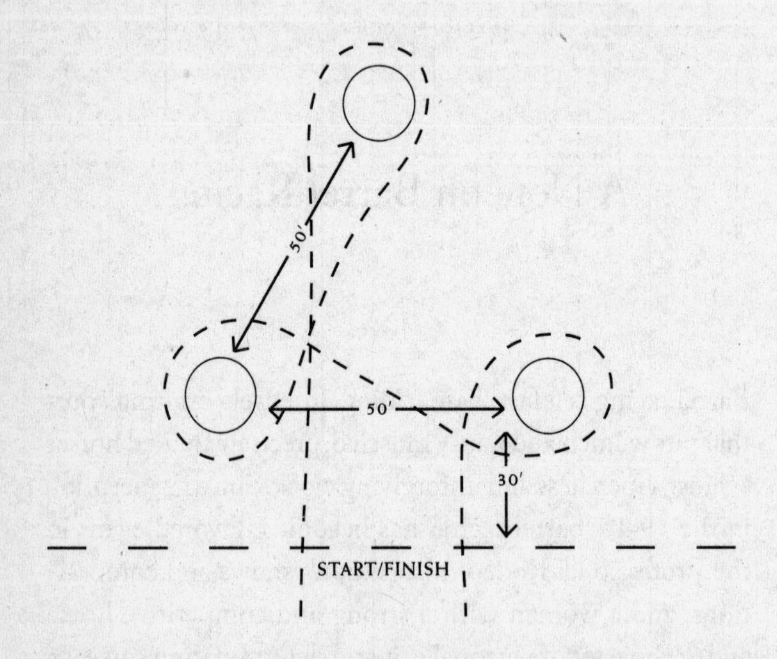

Consistently winning barrel horses must have a tremendous ability to accelerate and the ability to handle acutely tight turns in both directions at a full gallop. Equally important is that the horses must be as competitive as their riders and must love the contest with equal fervor. There are many fast horses but very few top barrel horses. There must exist a communion between horse and rider to shave seconds—and tenths of seconds—off the clock. It's that partnership that makes barrel racing the very special sport that it is.

Breeding, raising, and training barrel-racing horses is a large and competitive business, and the price asked for a finished (completely trained) horse can easily top twenty-five thousand dollars. But part of the beauty of the sport is that a horsewoman with enough drive, ability, and patience on a five-hundred-dollar grade horse that wants to win as badly as his rider does can be counting her prize money while her colleagues glumly load their multi-thousand-dollar mounts into their trailers.

Paige Lee Elliston reflects her keen understanding of the horse/rider relationship in her writings. She has written many novels in the general market and is the author of numerous short stories and articles. She lives in Rochester, New York.